THE FORTUNATE

Finn Fairlane

The FAIRLANE Series

THE FORTUNATE

Finn Fairlane

NICK SAVAGE

4 Horsemen
Publications, Inc.

4 Horsemen
Publications, Inc.

4 Horsemen Publications, Inc.
1497 Main St. Suite 169
Dunedin, FL 34698
4horsemenpublications.com
info@4horsemenpublications.com

Cover and typesetting by S. Casagrande
Editor 4 Horsemen Publications, Inc.

Library of Congress Control Number: 2022939165

Paperback ISBN-13: 978-1-64450-629-5
Audiobook ISBN-13: 978-1-64450-627-1
Ebook ISBN-13: 978-1-64450-628-8

DEDICATION

To Kris. You continue to inspire me.

Table of Contents

CHAPTER 1

Epic

I 've been told if you want to do something, get out there and do it. Don't wait for things to happen. Don't wait for things to come to you. They won't because you have to make things happen. So, I did. It's what I've always done. I create and help others create. Right now, I'm watching this thing I helped create—this living being that breathes on its own, unsteady on its infant legs, is unsure of what direction it wants (or is able) to move. But as it grows and matures, it finds its way. Its legs become steady, and it stands firm. It plays the music it helped to create through the conduit known as Spear Fist—the music from their fourth album, *Badaboom*.

I helped create that entity. I am a very proud parent, but it has grown. It is angry, screaming and cursing—and everyone loves it.

This creature that speaks to society—whispering to listeners' souls and inspiring them—some call it a rock band, others a music group. I call the creature's musical offspring records. I must nurture it and help it get to where it needs to go. Like a baby, it must be hand-held and guided. It must be led through the tour planning and nights of travel. It must learn the steps to the nightly performance: the setlist, the solo breaks, the song intros. That's our next step: the tour.

People may think that without the members, the music doesn't exist, but it does. It has always existed, laying all in wait for the right events to wake it up and usher it forth. Then, once the music is here, it never goes away. It lives on forever, not just through the albums, downloads, and radio waves, but with every impression it creates on a listener: the in-depth discussions about the meaning of a song; the older, life-long fan imparting musical wisdom that is Rush on some bright-eyed youth tapping the beat as he listens to *2112* for the first time; the long-haired, teenage boy in his Iron Maiden T-shirt, flannel, and ripped jeans learning the chords to "Powerslave" on his new Fender. In this instance, however, people are experiencing it live. The record release party is hugely successful, and I couldn't be happier. The current record label is here enjoying cocktails as they smooth talk possibilities with bigger labels. Potential tour managers, publicists, band managers, you name it … they are all here. The next step is happening right now.

It is all so beautiful. New life is rearing its head, and people are liking what they see and hear. It's music to the fan's ears. Many, many new fans and old fans are all enjoying the latest child of Spear Fist. Money in my pocket, cash in the band's pockets, but it all comes at a hefty price. There's a piper to be paid in order to produce something that will not be forgotten, to be part of that which will live on as its own. We've all seen it on MTV or VH1, or read about it in *Spin*, *Kerrang*, or *Rolling Stone*, the suicides and overdoses of the greatest musicians to ever live: Morrison, Jones, Joplin, Hendrix, Cobain. The harsh reality is that there's more to that list than just the few 27 Club members rattled off, more that don't belong to that club: Cornell, Bennington, Hide to name but three.

But the price is also paid behind the scenes. It's what happens after the lights have dimmed that lead up to the hotel room destruction, fights with fans, or band member brawls played out on the nightly news or MTV, back when it was about music with the great Martha Quinn feeding it to us, bit by bit. The screaming matches and thrown fists behind the veil, the smashed drum sets, split guitar necks, cracked bass bodies, bloody noses, and broken bones; the snide comment made by someone thought of as a friend that ignited the spark that led to the crimson mess; the loved ones left behind in some small town to move out to L.A., New York, Chicago, or wherever it was that first caused the lonesome trail of estranged family and friends. The overdoses don't start with peer pressure presented to them by some cheesetastic actor from a high school video warning about the danger of drugs in health class.

It begins without anyone noticing. It's some seemingly mundane moment that goes almost unnoticed that starts it all. But a piper must be paid for the way I left Faith and Viv unanswered on the patio. Driving off, leaving behind two women you claim to love doesn't go without repercussions. The rekindling of a flame nearing twenty years old doesn't come without cost, and, much like a cable company, doesn't forget the hidden charges and fees.

Those lucky enough to make it out the other side alive, sanity intact, get to see the music live on and take a shape all its own—actually enjoy the spoils of victory. Even more rare than not being written off as a has-been or never-was, or being crushed under the weight of everything, is the most precious of them all. If we are lucky enough; the loves we destroyed; the people who got left behind; the ones who mattered the most but wouldn't, or couldn't, stand in the way of the train wreck we call "pursuing the dream" are there at the end of it all. They stand with open arms as we crawl out from the wreckage of our success.

The band is on stage now, lights shining down on them. All the guys are in top form as the music blares forth from the amplifiers. The bassist, Neil, is uncharacteristically not standing off to the side, playing in some shadow. His energy carries him from one side of the stage to the next, over and over again, as his long curly hair trails behind like the tail of a comet. The sweat flies off Gregg as he hits drum skin after drum skin after drum skin. The veins in his arm course with as much blood as they can carry to make sure he delivers the boom of the bass drum in perfect timing and that each cymbal crash rings out with as much energy as the first in the set. Vincent rocks out his guitar riffs, showing his baby off to the world, and the world is eating it up.

D.B. is soaking in all the energy from the audience and putting it back out in his performance. The light glistens off the sweat of his brow as it drips onto the stage under him. D.B. screams word after word into the chrome microphone shining under the lights, helping bring this infant to life so the audience will always remember. It's something that the audience will want to run out and buy and listen to over and over again until the song is so ingrained in their heads they won't even need the CD anymore. It will just play in their minds, every note of every instrument in perfect pitch and perfect time.

I smile as I watch the band up there. This is it. The moment we've been working for—Finn Fairlane and his band of metal men. This moment is what it's all about: all the blood, sweat, and tears; everyone and everything we left behind; the parts of ourselves lost in the making of this thing. The countless days of work that's involved, the hours locked away in a studio seeing the same four faces over and over, the lack of sleep or proper food—most people don't see it. They don't know because they can't know unless they're in it. It's not just cool jam sessions with hot girls draped over the amplifier. There's so much more than most people know. But I know. Spear Fist knows.

Standing at the archway to the stadium, listening to them, watching them with her head leaned against the metal trim, is perhaps the only person in my life who knows how hard the music industry is without being in it herself. A melancholy smile hangs on her face as she stares toward the men on stage. A distant look in her eye, searching for answers to her life's mysteries; perhaps trying to figure out if either of our dreams would have come true if we didn't have the end we had. Maybe she is trying to figure out if her dreams have ever come true. But it is the sum of our experiences that make us who we are.

When I first met her, she was a much more strait-laced businesswoman-to-be. Even her admitted growing dislike of that field wouldn't necessarily have pushed her out of it. She may have made more of herself and settled down with a guy. Who knows? Had I not met her, maybe I wouldn't have ever been pushed to do what I have done. She has been my muse, and no one can be certain there would have been someone else. All I can do right now is watch her watch them and wonder what runs through her mind.

She turns her head and looks down the row of seats to this section's other entrance—to me. Her smile grows for a moment as she stares. She gives her head a couple of slow, determined shakes. There's a thought in there. I wish to the heavens above that I knew what it was. No one shakes their head unless they are thinking of an idea that requires a response. But I don't know why her smile grew. I can ponder forever and still not know. But after her smile has grown from ear to ear, her eyes light up. Her slow indication of a "no" stops. Her determined shake turns into a nod, one deliberate nod.

I nod back and return to watching the show. D.B. on stage, mic in hand, sings his heart out. Sweat pours off his entire body. He high fives a few people standing in the front row. I watch as I see our baby come to life up there, in front of a packed house.

A tap on my shoulder pulls me out of the trance and back to reality. A simple phrase is uttered, and the voice belonging to it is not Faith's. No, that would make it simple and pleasant. It's Vivian's (Viv's) voice that indicates her presence. I do love the sound of her voice. Though at this moment, all I want to do is enjoy the show, enjoy the party, enjoy this moment, and enjoy this night for all the work we put into it. I would like to relish in it for a while. But I hear Viv say, "Hey." So, I turn to face the music.

I attempt to force a smile for her, except there's too much on my mind. No smile emerges. The simple thought of not wanting to deal with her right now, not wanting to feel the fallout of recently passed events. I just wish she would see my intentions without me having to tell her them. I hate sounding like an ass-hole, but I guess if I sound like one while saying what's on my mind, even if she knew what I wanted without saying it, I'd still be an asshole—if only by intention. I just want to relish the moment; savor this moment of perfection, for these moments are few and quickly fleeting. In that regard, I guess it has fleeted. So let the music play. I shall face it with gusto.

"Hey, Viv. Nice to see you here." I keep it generic to not add to her ammo.

A chuckle from her indicates pleasantry, I hope. "Cut the quaint. I told you I'd be here. You think you leaving me with Faith, not answering either of us, is the worst thing that could have happened?" she fires at me.

"Yes," I say, immediately realizing the size of my ego. "No. Well, it wasn't a nice thing to do."

"No, it wasn't nice. But it's done. It also wasn't fair of either of us to corner you like that." Viv smirks.

I don't respond, not because I don't have anything to respond with but for all the shitty things I've done in my life, calling her out on something like that would be hypocritical. So, I nod, as I often do, and turn back to the show.

She leans against the wall, resting half against it and myself, her head on my shoulder as we watch the crowd. I've always enjoyed watching the crowds. There's your usual assortment of headbangers and mosh pit participants, but I like searching for the ones who feel the music on a higher level—not the guy in the pit who's so drunk he sways in there like a 'roided-out bodybuilder. Forget that guy. He's just blowing off steam from the fact he's got anger issues even outside the pit and knows it. Guys like that are just too stubborn to do anything about it. No, the one I want isn't in the mosh. He's close to the stage, protected by the buffer zone after the pit ends.

The fan whose focus is so zoned in on the stage and the sound that nothing else is in the room with them. Those fans are the people who need this the most. The kids in the mosh pit just need a release for anger, same with the headbangers. Whatever their need for release is, it's justified, I'm sure: bad day at work, problems at home that won't calm anytime soon, relationships, the gamut of issues everyone faces at some time. But those people out there, listening and watching with laser focus, those people need the cathartic energy. They have a spiritual connection with the music that ensures what we did wasn't a passing fad, that it will help those in need now and in the future. Those are the ones who let our spirits live forever through our lyrics, our music, and our songs.

Viv looks at me as the song plays out its final cords. I stare at her, unsure what to say since the fallout was painless: no punching, no crying, no thrown sticks or stones. The aftermath felt more like the calm before the storm, but maybe that's the way life works sometimes. The fallout is just there, an afterthought, something that exists in the background of our thoughts and minds. Sometimes, sometimes not.

I feel a hand wrap around my waist from the other side and slide toward Viv, which means it isn't Viv's hand. I turn to see Faith. Both women are not just within touching distance but are touching. Something feels wrong. Where's the other shoe? When's it going to drop and how hard? For the moment, I enjoy the silence among us and watch the event as the next song starts. I feel they understand what I did, what I had to do to get this to happen. The shoe will drop, just not now.

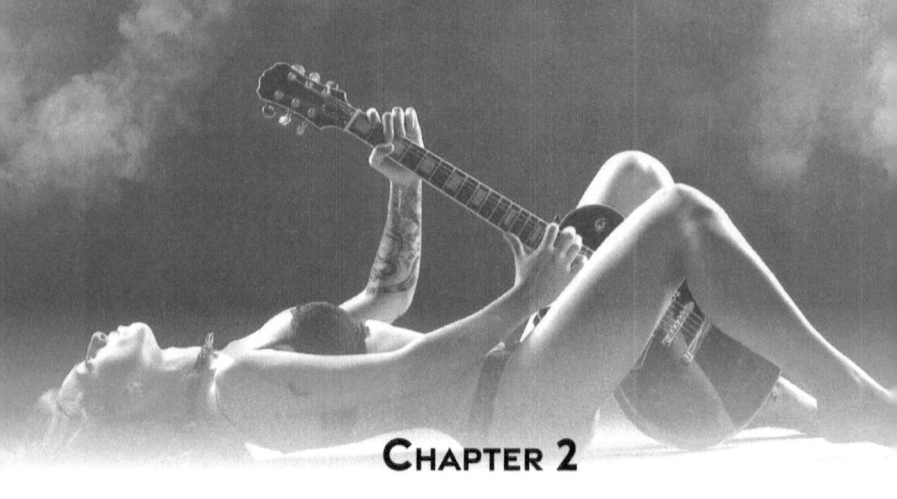

CHAPTER 2

*Can't Getcha Out
of My Mind*

There are significant moments in life that happen, and you have no choice but to feel yourself there, caught up in the moment, taking it all in: moments where you think you understand the impact of what is happening—moments when I stand off to the side, observing, watching, taking it all in, but my idea of the situation, my perceived comprehension of the events surrounding me, is not even close to what is actually transpiring. Sometimes what you see, what you think you are experiencing, is miles away from what is actually happening. The record release party had me basking in the warmth of what I had helped create: the event, the music, the surrounding atmosphere—all seemed calm after the storm as I looked onward to the stage. So, of course, I didn't see what was happening while I had my back turned. I didn't see the storm brewing quietly behind me.

It is a new night out with D.B., Vincent, Neil, and Gregg: no strumming guitars to make girls swoon, nor talks of upcoming albums; no new swooning fans for me to sweet talk into some carnal act behind bushes. The storm of this record is over, and not only did we survive, but we prevailed. So, we celebrate. As celebratory occasions call for, we decide to check out a new spot, to break the routine and start something new—some place called Taps & Corks, an unpredictable location that is, at any given time, either dead quiet or raucously boisterous and loud. But that doesn't matter since the pool table is decent and the tap selection is one of the best in the area. It's something of a hidden, local gem, far enough away from Orlando proper to not get too many weekend warriors but close enough to have the regulars night after night like a degenerate, drunken Cheers.

We all sit outside, under the Edison LED-lined, horseshoe awning at our wobbly wooden table and chairs. We sip on our local craft IPAs, laughing and joking around. The Orlando area after dark is always whispering a welcoming hello with a gentle breeze that whisks away the toils of the day on an otherwise quiet night.

"No, no, no," I say in defense against some half-heard question as Neil takes careful, cautious steps toward us, carrying a round of shots. "I've said it before, and I'll say it again: whether it was a one-night stand or some form of relationship, I've never had sex with a woman I didn't love on some level."

The guys laugh at that and wave me off.

"So, you're telling me," D.B. pipes in, "that you've never just nailed a girl to get your rocks off with no sort of emotional attachment at all?"

"Yes. But I think you all misunderstand what I say," I retort.

"First, take a shot," Neil says, setting down a round of shots.

"Fine," I say, tapping the table with the shot glass, then downing the crappy tequila. "It's not that I've been in love with every girl I've banged. I'm saying I've loved them on some level. It's not some Disneyfied-over and unrealistic romanticism that's been drilled into me from watching one too many princess stories."

"Then what is it?" Vincent chimes in.

"It's why waste your time with someone just to get your rocks off if there's no connection at all. I could use a crusty sock for that. Make connections on as deep a level as you can, every encounter you make, for as long as the encounter lasts," I explain.

"Deep," D.B. thinks aloud.

"Not really, but thanks. Life is too short to waste on anything else," I finish.

I think they all understand my words. It's why they write music. It's why they create what they create—to make connections with people on some level regardless of having met them or not, just connections through music. They're connections on a more profound level than looking cool with an axe in your hands and girls swooning over you as you stand in front of a mic; it's why we all write music.

It feels nice to get back to where we all once were, where we all once belonged, but there's something in the air, in the breeze that gently flows by; an almost stinging sensation whose irritation is just annoying enough to not ignore but whose source you can't trace. Maybe it's the betrayal of our day-of-the-week fried food restaurant to this place that pecks at me. Maybe. Perhaps it is something more.

A red Mustang pulls up. We all turn heads, like paparazzi at a red-carpet event, to see who exits the car and who they might be wearing, except none of us really give a crap about fashion. The source of the subtle, annoying stinging sensation reveals itself as the driver's door opens—Jeanine. She emerges from her car and waves at Gregg. The passenger door opens, and a soothing balm to relieve the sting in the name of Faith steps out.

The week since the release party has been unsettling, not that anything has happened but that's the unsettling part. Nothing has happened. Faith and I haven't talked. Nor have Viv and I. I know we all have lives, but there's an eerie feeling in the air that everything is not all right, one which I will try not to worry about tonight. Alcohol and paranoia are not good friends.

The horseshoe-style patio is great because it is both intimate and open. Small groups can all fit without being on top of each other and large groups can gather while still being comfortable. Faith and Jeanine make their understated entrance with a simple hello to everyone and take their seats, Jeanine on Gregg's lap and Faith next to me. She sits close to me as an acknowledgment of sorts but not as close as I'd like. Not that I want her on top of me dry humping away or anything, but a tad closer as an unspoken statement that we have history. Where she sits, it feels like a drinking buddy copped a squat there. I don't want to overthink the situation any more than I just have, so I turn my focus back to the moment with friends.

After an hour or two more of enjoying the night's celebration, Gregg directs everyone's attention to himself. The joyous night turns silent as he stands for an apparent announcement. Raising his glass, we all follow suit.

"This album, creating it, recording it, and releasing it, has been an unbelievable experience. I couldn't have joined the Spear Fist family at a better time or on a better album. It's been a helluva ride! You made me feel at home. Thank you."

D.B., Vincent, and Neil all nod while D.B. throws in a wink of reciprocation.

"And I want to thank Finn … for his time and dedication to us, to the album, to helping us create something more. And because of this, we are going on a North American tour. I'm very grateful."

He turns to Jeanine and says, "But through all this, I know that you, baby, have been by my side and have helped calm my nerves on more than a few occasions. I know that you have helped push not only me but others as well." He turns to me and nods. I nod back. "In this thing we call life, I could not have asked for a better woman to be at my side." He looks around and gets down on one knee. "I know this isn't the most romantic spot to do this, but … I don't want this to change. Jeanine Siubhal, will you always stand by my side and be the inspiration in everything I do?" I see the surprise on her face accompanied by an ear-to-ear smile as he pulls out a ring, but I'm not close enough to see if it's a ten-karat ring encrusted with stolen jewels from ancient Arabia or something he got from Hot Topic.

To me, this moment isn't about them. I turned away before I could see, what I am guessing is, her shaking her head, jumping up and embracing him in some Hallmark-fashion. No, I'm no longer watching the happy couple but am instead staring at Faith. There is a distance in her eyes as she watches the moment, trying to be happy for her sister—a fight against the happiness she feels for her sister, knowing the struggle that comes with the life she is about to (hopefully) permanently enter. She senses me staring at her and looks at me, her eyes turning to a sad sullenness. She gives a weak, fast fading smile, the corners of her lips dying as soon as they spring to life. Faith shakes her head no. Not a full shake, though, but enough so that I can see it while sitting next to her. An answer to an unasked question, but what is the question she is answering?

Jeanine and Gregg share a joyous kiss. I hope the happiness they feel now lasts through the nights of late shows, long travel, the frustration of writing, and the complex and sometimes resentful mind of the creative person.

I still stare at Faith, trying to read her mind and hear the question in her mind that she answered. Is she saying no to their engagement lasting, or no to the thought of me ever doing such a thing to her? My attempts at mind-reading are cut short. Faith stands up, says her half-hearted congrats, walks away from the crowd, enters the bar, and takes a seat at the counter. I hear the cosmic voice in my head tell me, "Go get her." I follow suit with sincere congrats and they are wholehearted, for this is a joyous moment. I may not be the biggest fan of Jeanine's, but she wasn't wrong when she blew up my relationship with Viv. Plus, she makes Gregg happy. I head to the bar and grab a seat next to Faith. My back to the outside tells her with body language that I am here for her.

She turns to me as I sit. "Seeing a car crash in Florida is not something you wonder if you'll see, just when you'll see it. When you see it happening, you know it's not going to be good, which means it becomes how bad is this going to be."

"But isn't that life? No matter what car you drive, accidents are accidents. They happen. So, why not have someone in your passenger seat who makes you smile? Someone who makes you feel like a better version of yourself? He's a good guy, Faith. Better than most out there."

She downs an entire double bourbon neat in one gulp. "Damn it, Finn. You know the road they're headed down."

"No. That's the thing; we don't know. We know the metaphorical car they'll be driving and who will be driving. We don't know who will be riding in the backseat or alongside them. We don't know. We can only guess based on our experience. Since no two experiences are alike, it means a different answer from each person you ask," I state.

Maybe she's right. Perhaps she knows what will happen, but that would be just a coincidence. Maybe she can see the future, but more realistically she's worried for her sister. Perhaps she realizes that things could have been different for her, different for us. But as much as I try not to ponder on these things, it's in my nature to wonder. If she is still so upset by the thought of it all, then perhaps there still is hope. That ever-shining light in the distance that we all navigate by praying it doesn't lead us astray: hope.

So, with hope in my heart, I speak. "We could drive together. Hop in the same car and see where the road takes us."

She smiles and points at me with a suspicious finger. "We've traveled that road before, Finn. And it was rough and broke us." She sips a new double bourbon that is placed in front of her.

"But we're different. Stronger than we were twenty years ago."

"See, that's the thing. We might be stronger, but something tells me, hell, shows me that you are no different." Faith's words sting my heart.

I have to try and soothe the pain. "Those were ... a series of unfortunate, and unplanned, events. Things happened. I want this, and something inside tells me you do too, despite your outward reservations."

"Perhaps you're right. But right now, at this moment, I'm not thinking about that. About us. Right now, I'm drinking to not think about my sister or the road she's about to travel down. I'm drinking because you might be right. I'm drinking because of her." Faith polishes off another double bourbon, sets the glass down, and stumbles back out to the crowd. As she does, Viv walks by, giving a friendly hello. Faith, however, makes a feeble attempt to smile and wave.

Of course, this is happening right now. Why wouldn't it be happening now? Every time I want to talk or have a moment with Faith to try and put back together some of the broken pieces of our past, something happens. In this instance, it's Viv. Not that I should be too upset since I do love her. Maybe love is too strong a word. I do care greatly for her. (Isn't that the Hallmark card you want from someone? "Dear blah blah, times with you have meant the world to me. I care for you greatly, but because I'm emotionally stunted, I can't tell if it's love. Sincerely, Ass-face." The card cover will have a rose on it.)

She is an amazing woman who cares a great deal for me as well. She didn't walk out when she learned the whole truth of my past with Faith. She still came to the release party after I left her unanswered on the restaurant patio. She is here tonight. The one thing that I don't understand is why Jeanine did that to her friend. I know why she did it—to get me to concentrate, though doing that to her friend was uncool. But I digress. She's here right now. The reality is things with Faith seem to be stalled on a deserted road with no hope of being fixed (at the moment). I shall see what Viv wants from me.

She plops down on the bar stool next to me, and before turning to me with that unsure look in her eye, she orders a Sailors & Sprite. I wait for her to speak. Not that I don't have anything to say, but I don't want her to feel pressured into some sort of banter if silence is what she prefers.

"We need to talk," Viv starts.

Or not; Viv wants to talk. Now my mind starts racing … pacing … wondering. Hell, can you do all three at the same time? I'm not sure, but if a mind can, mine is. Why is it I always feel like I'm in these unfortunate situations that I didn't put myself in? Am I being broken up with twice in the same night?

"I'm listening," I say, sipping my Boom Juice IPA. She doesn't immediately start speaking. Her pressed lips contort as she searches for her words. Her scrunched nose is making her look far more adorable than she wants. She looks so innocent at this moment, like a child vampire in a goth-horror movie right before a kill. It has me on guard.

"We talked. Faith and I, at the Spear Fist show," she says.

I give her a corrective look that sets her on a quick rapid-fire correction, "Record release party, album bash, whatever. We talked." She slows down again. "You're a wonderful person, a good, helluva guy. But you're a wreck. You're a mess of a person." She scrunches her face for a half-second at something she just said. "Helluva guy? I don't say things like that. I don't even sound like myself right now."

I want to interrupt. I want to say something that will reverse this car crash happening in front of me. But I know it might be too late for that. If it is, it is all my fault. I stare at the beautiful nose ring, snake bites, and melancholy stare that made me fall for her in the first place, hoping that somewhere in there is hope for me.

"We've had fun. A passionate, wild start. But this," Viv says, while her finger waves back and forth pointing at me and herself, "can't work. I want it to, though."

"Me too," I interject.

She puts up her hand to stop me from saying more as if, perhaps, my words could sway her. She won't let that happen.

"I know you do. You want it to work with me. But, not just with me. That's what hurts the most. That, despite everything, you still cling to what could be with Faith and not what is with me."

She pauses, the sadness in her eyes stopping her from saying what's next. My mind looks to the immediate future, in search of what could be coming. Is she walking away from everything, or will we still be friends? As if that ever really works. Her lips won't move. They try to open, but some unseen, powerful force keeps holding them shut.

She turns to her Sailors & Sprite and sucks it all down through the tiny, black stir straw. She slides it forward and motions for another before turning back to me. "I could have loved you. Like, truly, deeply, madly loved you, Finn. I was starting to, ya know. See, that's what hurts. Not falling for some rockstar I loved from my teen years. In the end, I don't care about that. I care about you, but you care about more than just me. Here's the rub: I deserve better. What makes this whole situation sad is that without me, you can care just for her. Without her, you'd still care for her. That's what hurts the most."

How am I supposed to respond? Do I tell Viv she is wrong when I know she's right? Do I beg and plead for her to stay when she's already made up her mind?

"You're the fortunate Finn Fairlane." She adds a bit of fake awe to my name. "You really are. Everyone, at one time or another, finds someone they think could love them. You have at least two women who, on some level, do love you. But you are just too stupid to see that and be with that love," she finishes as she swirls around in her bar chair to walk away.

"Wait," I plead.

She stops and turns around but doesn't walk back. "Don't worry. I'll still be around. I'm a glutton for punishment."

"So that's it?!" I say at a high enough volume that might be confused for yelling. We aren't exactly whispering anymore. The rest of the barflies are too drunk or involved in their own dealings to pay attention to our public display of affliction anyway. "That's all she wrote?!"

Viv laughs. "Is that ever all she wrote with you? Someday, after we're no longer intertwined, I'll retell the great Fairlane incidents of 2017, and no one will believe me. Maybe I'll start a journal so for all eternity there's proof that once upon a time this actually happened." She takes out her phone and snapshots a picture of me, stunned.

I watch as she opens the door to the outside world. I can see sadness mixed with overwhelming relief engulf her expression as she breathes in the warm night air. Her shoulders lift a little as if the weight of my world has lifted off her shoulders. "I'll see ya around, Finn."

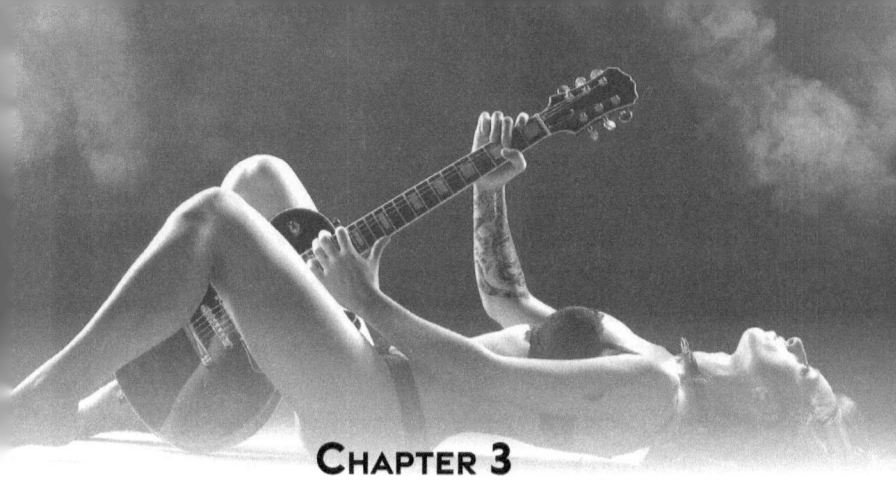

CHAPTER 3

Majestic

The times, they are a-changin', or at least they are for me. As they change, I find myself back where I started down here, standing in front of the greasy hamburger stand outside Old Town, chomping away on fast food as I listen to the world around me. The sounds of locals hitting on some attractive tourist from some random city, the families seated nearby as they discuss the past day's events, laughter and screams from the rides all surround me—they swirl about my ears and my mind, trying to feed me some ounce of inspiration. I need to hear an anecdote to motivate me. I need to see some pure emotion in someone's eyes or smile to guide me, some sign within the cosmos that grabs my attention and steers me toward greatness.

The upcoming tour, and now Gregg's wedding, need to come together. This tour can't be some chump tour playing basement bars and rural barns. It needs to be bigger. It needs to launch their status in the industry to more of a household name. The wedding has to be something that won't be overshadowed by the impending tour. If the wedding fails to go off, or doesn't happen for some unknown reason, the tour will not happen. Of course, it can't be as extravagant as the tour. I must keep all the tour plans away from Gregg. I must put aside any old grievances I have with Jeanine and work toward a common goal. Not that I'm involved in the wedding. Hell, Faith hasn't asked me to be her date, and I wouldn't just assume to be her date. So, unless the band invites me, I might not even be going. But back to my point: musicians implode. I need to make sure that doesn't happen.

A mental checklist of the things I need to do: realistic tour dates, travel plans, accommodations, band lineup for each stop, marketing the tour, merch ideas. There's a whole list I'm not remembering right now. I can't. My mind isn't focusing. That to-do list seems insurmountable, in part because I can't zone in on any one point. My mind is playing leapfrog, jumping from bullet point to bullet point but never lingering long enough to flesh out any details. Something isn't right at this particular moment. I look around at the tourists and locals in their sandals and shorts. I see teenagers finding young lust. Hell, I even think I hear the same girly-man screaming on the Vomatron from my first night here, but it's just not the same. Maybe it's that the night breeze is a little cooler. Perhaps it's because I've become intertwined, on some level, with this great city. Maybe it's simply that you can't go home again. Home, in this instance, being my first Orlando muse.

I try to find any inspiration as I look around. The giant, neon entrance shines its color at me, but it's coming in dull. The drones of conversations around me ring distant. Everything around me seems far more mundane than my first encounter. The people are all having fun, but it all seems as generic as the gift shops that line West Irlo Bronson Memorial Highway. This isn't working for me, none of it is. It all falls flat and uninspired. Any artist knows when he can't or doesn't feel the inspiration surrounding him, it's time to move on.

Making things happen, making music happen, is what I've done for almost twenty years. It hasn't always been easy, and it hasn't always been fun. But when you want to do something, whether it be making some music or becoming a doctor, you do what you need to do to make your dream a reality. You give it your best shot, all your attention, and things get sacrificed: relationships fall apart, loves that could have been great—groovy kinds of loves—pass you by, family grows distant, friends get left behind. All are a means to an end, but it doesn't happen overnight. It doesn't miraculously fall into your lap without sacrifice. And it definitely doesn't happen without inspiration.

Back at my home studio, I riffle through some old lyrics I wrote. I find a few sets whose words still hold meaning and relevance. Looking over those, I listen to some old instrumental recordings I had saved on my computer. I'm searching for something, anything, that says my time down here will be worth more than the first three-and-a-half months, some notion that gives me direction on where to go next. Anything at all. Again, though, I find myself empty, staring at old, unpublished writings that do not stand the test of time. Looking at some of these, I'm not sure they had a shelf life of even a month. I need something, and I need it fast. Deadlines wait for no man. As such, I do what I do. I get in my car and drive toward inspiration.

There's no better place to find inspiration when your usual wells have dried up than a record store. Now I'm not talking FYE, or any corporate, overpriced, vague resemblance of a Spencer's-turned-CD store. I mean a real record store. One run by a few tatted dudes who have lost and worn out more cassettes and vinyl than most will ever own. A store with aisle after aisle of CDs and stuff that spins at 33 & 1/3. Park Ave CDs is one such place. Now it might not be the size of Amoeba Records in Hollywood, but the selection is still damn impressive. Hell, I haven't been to Amoeba in a while. It may not exist anymore but if it does, make it a must-stop on your next Cali trip. But in Orlando, Park Ave CDs is the place to buy.

It is here I find myself trying to flip through vintage vinyl until I stumble upon something so beautiful, so jaw-droppingly eye-catching, so wonderfully unique that I have to have it. I have to listen to what it has to say to me, and I must ingest everything it has to offer so I can give back to the universe something that can only hopefully compare in greatness. As my mind can't stand the thought of it anymore, I catch out of the corner of my eye something so beautiful, so wondrous, that I couldn't ignore it. My head turns to get a full view. I'd say this beauty is about twenty-five years vintage, dressed in torn, faded jeans, and a baggy, home-torn tank top from an old Skinny Puppy tour, with ombre hair pulled back in a long ponytail. She has on such simple attire, and it is beyond sexy. Before I can even fully take in all there is to her, she looks at me and smiles. My heart pounds within my chest. She wasn't supposed to see me staring. This wasn't a leer, just a view of admiration that went on a second too long.

"So, which is better in your opinion?" she says, holding up two CDs. I set my selection of vinyl against a support column and make my way to her. My mind races about the possibility of the conversation about to happen. I am not falling in love with her at first sight. My reverence for her is far more aesthetic. Beauty can spark creativity. It happens every day in a sunrise somewhere for a poet or a new paint job on an old car that moves a mechanic to tune up his old Corvette. As I walk the twenty or so steps around the aisle to her, my mind is already starting to simmer with new ideas for songs, locations for tour stops I haven't thought of before now, stage setups, new merch ideas, and more. Everything else that has been slumbering away in my mind is waking up, stretching out the sleep that had overcome it, and is beginning to move about.

She hands me *Jungle of The Midwest Sea* by Flatfoot 56 and *Smash the Windows* by The Tossers. A quick glance, I give them both back to her, and say, "Get 'em both."

She looks at me for a second and nods her head. "I like that idea."

"If you like raw energy, check out The Pogues, Pink Fairies, Heavy Metal Kids, or Days N Daze. Those guys all deliver. Not that Flatfoot or The Tossers don't," I offer up.

"Thanks." She smiles. "Any other suggestions?"

"If you really want an experience, pick up Nick Cave and The Bad Seeds," I add.

"Murder Ballads is my favorite." She surprises me with that response.

"Name's Finn," I finally introduce myself.

"Jacquelyn. Nice to meet you, Mr. Finn." She extends a hand.

I gently shake hers. "Just Finn. Finn Fairlane. No mister."

"Alliterative, like a superhero. Peter Parker. Bruce Banner. Matt Murdock. Clark Kent-Man of Steel. Finn Fairlane—man of music." She smiles.

She obviously doesn't know who I am, or was, which makes me wonder why she's talking to me. Maybe it is just for a good recommendation. Whatever the reason, I'm happy to talk.

I notice a look in her eye. She's searching for something in mine. I don't know what it is she's searching for. I guess it must be the same look I give people, and probably just gave her, to see if they recognize me and want to be in close proximity for some superficial reason or if they actually just want to talk. I do know that if she is looking for a music recommendation, she's probably not directly involved in the industry or a rabid fan of any particular genre, which means I don't know her or why she's giving me that look. Could she be just a regular person who happened to stop me in my comfort zone? A welcome stranger to discuss things within my wheelhouse? Wouldn't that be a nice change of pace?

"So, are good music recommendations your only superpower, or are there more?" she continues with a playful laugh.

"That and a great ability to screw things up right before my eyes," I say with an odd hand wave like I'm performing a magic trick.

"Well, Finn. That doesn't sound like a fun superpower." She adjusts the tension of her ponytail as she begins to eye the register.

"It's not, but the demolition is a sight to see." I try to save face.

"Hmm. I see. Well, thank you for the many bands I shall be checking out. You seem to know your way around a music store." She starts toward the checkout.

"I try. Enjoy." I smile back, giving her a two-finger salute and a wink.

I grab the selection of records I had leaned against the column and head to the register. While paying, I look around at the customers in the aisles and the guys behind the counter. These people are why I continue to do what I do. It's nice to be here. It's nice to have met Jacquelyn. Moments like these confirm that all the relationships I have had and subsequently blown up weren't all for nothing. While the immediate result is more often than not a destructive one, the things that grow from the ashes are, in the big scheme of things, even greater.

New tunes in hand, I say a silent goodbye to Park Ave CDs, turn my car's ignition on, and check my mirrors where I spy that next to me, listening to her new, choice picks, is Jacquelyn. She turns down the volume and waves for my attention.

"I have an extra ticket to a show this weekend at House of Blues over at Disney Springs. My way of saying thank you for the help."

"That's a very kind gesture for a simple recommendation. Won't the person you were supposed to bring be upset?" I pry.

"Subtle, Finn, but there's no one in that sense. Assuming that's what you're implying. They were just a gift." A perfect reply from a seemingly perfect woman.

I chuckle and half-smile, brushing back my hair with my hand. "Sounds fun." I grab a piece of paper and pen, get her number.

Before I can roll my window all the way up, she shouts, "Don't you wanna know who's playing?"

"What?"

"The concert. This weekend. Don't you wanna know who you're going to see?" she asks.

Shaking my head, I shout back, "Not really. Any concert is better than no concert."

She smiles at my response, rolling up her window. Between my new records and my upcoming weekend rendezvous, I would call today a success.

I drive away smiling at my fortune, ideas flowing and springing to life. This was just what I needed. Serendipity, if ever there was such a thing. Now, as there are still a few things I need to pick up, I head on over to my next stop.

CHAPTER 4

Delirious

The weather has shifted since earlier, so now the temperature is dipping into the chilly, high fifties. Quite a drastic drop for Florida, but being from the Midwest and New York, I am still warm, though slowly acclimating to the weather. By this time next year, I'll be cold. People, the tourists and the locals alike, don't seem to mind the chilly cold here in The City Beautiful. That's the joy of living in a tourist town. When everyone looks like they are on vacation, the warm tourists, the acclimating local transplants, and chilled local natives alike all blend seamlessly together to make this city always comfortable and the epitome of endless summer.

I step out of the coziness of my Grand Am into the nibbling cold, walk past the replica *Back to The Future* DeLorean and into, in my humble opinion, Orlando's best music store, George's Music.

As soon as I walk in, the walls of guitars off to the right that usually call out my name are drowned out by a loud, rambunctious, pink-and-black-haired girl off to the left, testing microphones at noise levels I imagine Huey Lewis telling her through his megaphone she's "just too darn loud." But there's this raw energy to her voice, one that can both hold a key and sound like she's about to spew blood from grated vocal cords.

I head over to watch as she screams in various pitches, with different vocal effects all emanating from within her. The words she sings I do not recognize, perhaps they are her own. She looks up at me with crazy eyes outlined in haphazard black mascara and clumped eyeshadow. She hands the mic back to the salesman and steps toward me.

"Whatcha starin' at?" she sneers.

"Talent."

She chuckles a bit, but her guard stays up, a feature manifested in spiked wrist guards. "Nice pickup line, bub, but I like innies, not outies."

I give a whole body laugh at her presumptuous response. "Outies and innies. Nice euphemism. Not why I am standing here, though."

She stops her shopping and gives me a moment. "Then why ya here?"

"Were those lyrics your own?"

"Yeah. Why?" she says, epitomizing the nineties image of the overly defensive new adult.

"I liked them. What's the name of your band?" I try to help her relax before she has an aneurysm.

She gives a quick breath out and shakes her head. "Don't have one at the moment."

"What? A band or a band name?" I retort.

"Band," she snaps back.

"Too bad. You've got some real potential." I start to turn away from her, slow and deliberate.

Her brow furrows, eyes narrowing to needle points aimed at me. "What the hell does that mean? Potential?"

"Potential means you have the qualities and, hopefully, capacity to do something greater," I jab.

"Listen, jerk. Don't patronize me. I know what potential means," she jabs back, poking me with a sharp, threatening finger.

"You're the one who asked what it means." I hope for a response.

She doesn't bite.

Before stepping away, I bait her by saying, "I mean, I'm setting something up, and from what I heard, I thought well ... nevermind."

She steps toward me with an outstretched arm. "Wait. I'm working with a band, but we're replacing a guy."

"So, you do front a group." I smirk.

"Yeah. Sorta," she says, averting her eyes.

"Why are you replacing a member?" I keep my tone innocent.

She gets agitated, shifting back and forth on her feet while tapping her hand against her opposite arm. "Look, bub. He didn't understand the metaphor and persisted a little too hard. You got a problem with that?"

I throw up my hands to show I mean no harm. "Hey. Good enough for me. How's the search comin'?"

"Nothing yet," she says, defeated.

"You put an ad out for one?"

"Damn." The defensiveness of her words protects her emotions. "No, not yet. Why the hell do you give a crap anyway?"

"You seem to not be having a good day. Give me your band name, site, whatever, and I'll contact you in a day or two."

"The Shit Machines," she says with a shit-eating grin.

"Seriously?" I try not to laugh. "You're called The Shit Machines?"

A hearty laugh escapes from within her, allowing her to relax for a minute. "Nope. Just thought it'd be fun to fuck with you a little."

I smile. "Nicely done. So?"

"So what?"

"So, what's your band's name?"

"Logan Square."

"Interesting name. How many albums?"

"Two. Working on the third." Her guard drops a little more as she describes her band.

"Do your albums have names or just colors associated with them?" I search her for a little more info.

"*Fistful of Nothing* was our first. *Punching Rosebuds* followed that," she says.

"*Punching Rosebuds*?" I pause between words, clearly missing something here.

The beginning of a sly smile forms as she holds up a fist and, with her other hand, curls her index finger tightly into her wrapped thumb like a tense okay sign. She proceeds to shove the fist through the two-fingered rosebud. "Sex sells. Even dirty sex."

I shake my head in amusement. "What's the title of your third album?"

"*Violent Relaxation*. Figured this one we'd keep less *Deep Throat* and veer toward astronomy references."

I don't want to overstay my welcome with her. Seeing that I do have my own things I need to accomplish, I extend my hand out for a handshake. "Thank you for your time. I'll be listening tonight and be in contact. What's your name?"

"Logan."

A light bulb goes off in my head. "Nice. Logan Square."

She smirks. "Not too dull there, mister..." She returns the handshake.

"Finn," I reply as I turn away. "Nice to meet you."

"Ya, you too."

I leave Logan be to stir in the momentary unsettling that is both her lousy day and potential for something greater. I gather the new strings, cables, the bass guitar I've been wanting, and a few new FX pedals so I can head back to my abode and create some musical genius.

At this point in the game with Spear Fist, I don't actually need to be creating new music for them at this moment, but I find the process of creation to be a cross-platform experience. It helps me figure out show lineups, plan trips from city to city, and create new music for future use. The hardest part for me is helping lineup bands to tour with, as not all groups do more than one leg. Yes, venues have their own booking agents, but I like to be more hands-on than some other people in the industry. I want to make sure things run as smooth as possible, even if it creates more work for me.

I rack up a few more thousand onto my credit card (if only for the points) and start loading up my car. On my way out the door, with the last armload of newly purchased goods, I turn back to Logan who is standing where we said our parting words, microphone in hand. On her face is, what I can only assume, the closest thing to a smile she has mustered in a long time. She's not doing anything either, just standing there in this awkward stare that looks like she's frozen in time. However, there's this look in her eye, a look that screams she couldn't give less of a shit about what she looks like in that moment. Something is going on inside her head that has gripped her and is holding her in that spot. She knows the thought is delicate, and any movement will cause the idea to flee. It is this level of self-comfort, of okayness, that makes for great stage presence.

She's not going to be one of those musicians who's up on stage worried about whether or not their bicep muscles look savage during the raging guitar solo their fingers are bleeding out when, a couple decades earlier, they were a skinny, lanky kid who had talent dripping off their chin. No, she won't be one of those. Musicians like that don't lose talent, just respect. It becomes about looks and sellability to them, not the music. I spent too many years doing that in my own way and losing respect for myself; I won't go there again. I know this Logan girl never will. Watching her stand frozen, oblivious about how others perceive her; that's what music is about, not giving a crap.

Whatever thought is playing out in her head must be a good, deep one. Something has struck a great chord in her head, and from the amount of time she's been thinking, it must be important. Hopefully, it's something to inspire her. Hopefully I helped with that.

Who knows? Maybe she does not know the source of her thought. She could be standing there, trying to figure out where the notion came from and what it all means. Either way it goes, in two days-time I'll be getting a hold of her, and if the thought took root enough in her, perhaps I'll hear about it. But now, I have work to do.

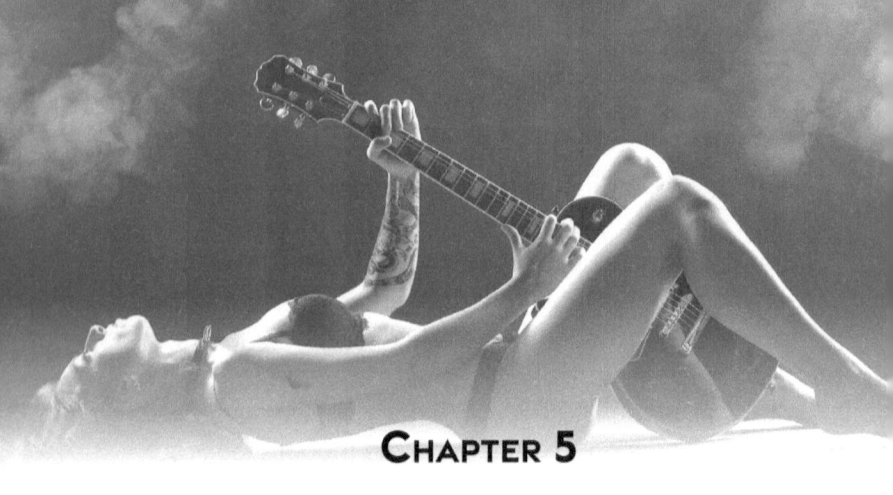

CHAPTER 5

Hazy Shade of Winter

Florida winters are an oxymoronic thing. Sure, from a technical standpoint, we have winter in so much as the season is marked on our calendars. Having lived in Chicago and NYC, I can tell you what we experience in Florida is not winter. It, at best, is a mild cooling off from the scorching summer days. The coldest parts of the nights will dip into the forties or even thirties, if it's terrible, but the days are still comfortably warm in the fifties, sixties, and seventies.

But that's the thing: cold can creep up on you out of nowhere too. What starts as a beautiful day in the high seventies or low eighties can sink down into the forties at night. If you're already out enjoying a night on the town, the cold strikes you unprepared. You're left chilly, without a jacket, flannel, or some piece of clothing with long sleeves to stave off the cold. The beginning of this winter has already been unseasonably cold. To be honest, it might still be late fall. Hell if I remember when each season starts.

I restring my guitars and new bass and get everything else in order. (I'm not wanting to wait three days for store set-up on an instrument that plays well off the wall.) Instead of picking up an acoustic guitar or bass and fiddling away, I open Bandcamp.com and search for The Shit Machines. I do this out of morbid curiosity to see if some other group of rejects already took the name. Behold, no one has been that brazen, but there are several records named in a similar vein. After my inquiring mind is satisfied, I search for Logan Square and pull up a discography of their first two albums.

I didn't think that the small-framed, pink-and-black-haired Logan, or rather the inner angst that was her, would lead such an interesting, eclectic combination of sounds. Best likened to a mixture somewhere between Faith No More's first two albums with Mike Patton and the sludginess of Alice in Chains or The Atlas Moth. It's an interesting mix that's pleasing to the ear and, at the same time, is utterly dissonant. Lot's of 7th's in the vocal harmonies and suspended chords, but among all that, the thing that sticks out the most, at least for me, are the lyrics: relevant, authentic, and intelligently written. The anger, the pain, the hope that lies within the words all have pointed directions and speak loudly of today's collective feelings.

Yes, I now know who I want on a lineup with Spear Fist on this tour (if only for a small leg). I am not in charge, though, so I have to run it past the guys or, at the very least, D.B. I shoot him a text asking to meet up, if for nothing more than a name drop for him to check, good conversation, and a beer with a friend, perhaps a word or two about Faith or Viv if he's heard anything. I write Logan a quick message via Bandcamp reminding her of our meeting and the usual courtesy of hoping she is okay. Now I wait and see if she gets back to me.

I find myself feeling a bit peckish as I drive to my meetup, so I reroute D.B. to a new destination. This way we can grab some food too. I change our stop to a Florida staple Tex-Mex joint called Tijuana Flats. The food itself is exceptional, with a hot sauce bar to boot. Speaking for myself, it's the excellent paint job of green, dripping goo around the door frames, and a sugar skull facing the cashier, taking up almost the entire height of the wall, that I find impressive. The hair on the sugar skull flows back to the entrance door. A handful of the acoustic ceiling tiles are hand painted by different local artists, making this company an artist haven of sorts. Doubly, it gives me the ability to eat and simultaneously be inspired.

The irony here is that despite my over-glorified intro to such a Florida favorite, my meal today is their signature queso dip and chips; it's a simple, delicious snack food to fuel my evening. As I take a seat at a high top table within arms-reach of the hot sauce, D.B. arrives and orders something much more substantial than I: a double meat steak burrito with extra jalapeños, beans, and rice, sure enough to dwarf my tray of chips—at least to the outside observer. To anyone who's eaten here, both meals are fit for a king.

We stand at the hot sauce bar, surveying the ten or so different flavors, all lined up from mild to hottest. As we gather our tiny cups of varying flavor hot sauces, the idea hits me for tour stops, a few festivals added in for a broader audience. For the single-stop nights, book a few different flavors of metal. Like the hot sauce bar, they are all sauces but at different degrees. We can add bands from hardcore, metalcore, thrash, black metal, doom metal, all different genres, and make a tour stop or two more of a day-long event than just an evening out.

While we wait for our food, we get straight down to business—the tour. "I met a girl named Logan who fronts Logan Square. They'd be great to do a few shows with. Have you given any thought to the tour? Who you guys want to tour with? What cities are a must? So on and so forth." I dive into the conversation.

He takes a sip of his blue Powerade. "Yes and no," he responds.

"Those are the two definitive answers to my question," I quip back.

"Yeah, of course. I have," D.B. restarts, "but we're already running into roadblocks." He gives me a look that is both irritated and annoyed, a look I have given many times before. I have an unnerving feeling I know the source of their newfound troubles.

"Jeanine?" I ask, already knowing the answer.

He nods, drinking another sip. His eyes wander upward, unsure of what to say next. He stares at ceiling tile after ceiling tile, pretending to study each one's artwork as if he's some ceiling art scholar, but I know what's running through his mind. It's the same thing that's run through all the minds of every entertainer at some point. He's starting to think that this guy who's only an album deep with the band, who meshes well with them and is talented on the skins, is now going to make every decision, musical or otherwise, based on how his counterpart will react to it. He'll think about what she would want, what she would say, and what she would tell him to do. D.B. is worried that all of Gregg's judgment will now defer to Jeanine. He's concerned about the guy behind the drums being effectively replaced by the girl behind him.

"What's happening?" I probe. "What's she done?"

"Finn!" a voice shouts from just outside their kitchen. A girl no more than twenty-two, with curly black roots into a faded red ombre, calls out my name. I raise my hand and say, "Here!" As she delivers my chips and queso, another girl of a similar age calls out, "Danny!" He follows suit, and she drops off his food. At last, we both get to eat. Hopefully this will quell him a tad.

"She wants to be married by the start of the tour," he lays it all out. "And a traditional wedding at that."

"Three weeks till they tie the knot? Five weeks total to plan? She's fuckin' nuts," I say, queso dripping down my chin. "She can't do all that planning and us finish planning the tour? Even planning a tour this fast borders on stupid!"

"It's interfering with practice. We're tight and all, but there's more to it than just the music. You know that," D.B. responds in an almost defeated manner.

I sit, eating queso-covered chip after queso-covered chip, eyes wandering around, trying to think: trying to figure out how I'm going to handle this without disrupting the delicate balance of the band, not break up Gregg and Jeanine, and also not further piss off

Faith in the process. I know Faith should be the last thing on my mind, not even weigh in as a factor to this equation, but like it or not, she's part of it, at least indirectly.

The next thing out of my mouth is the line every good person in my position says, the five little words that keep clients happy and things moving forward (at least momentarily): "I'll take care of it."

He nods through a bite of his burrito. A muffled "Thank you" escapes his mouth.

"It's what I do. So, bands?" I prod.

"A couple I have in mind, but I haven't contacted any of them yet. We've never done a full North American tour, just regional shit. Even our overseas tours were small in comparison," he rattles off, in an attempt to satisfy my question.

"No worries. I'll contact the bands—just give me their names," I say in an attempt to ease his mind. "Also, what sort of trust do you have with me just lining up some bands without needing to run them by you?"

"That's fine. You know your stuff. As long as you think they'll fit the bill, go for it. As for the bands I have in mind…" He starts rattling off a few bands I've never heard of before: Children of Dismay, Bereft, and Starkill in the Midwest; Spellcaster and Four Stroke Baron on the West Coast. But honestly, my mind is elsewhere. I imagine the talk I'm going to have with Jeanine. I'm thinking about whether Faith will be there as a witness, and if so, how I'm not going to come off the bad guy. I'm thinking about the conversation I must have with Gregg about Jeanine. But a thought occurs to me, one that has nothing to do with the music but still needs to happen before the tour: the bachelor party.

"Who's the best man?" I ask, changing the subject.

A smile crosses his face, hinting to the answer I suspected would exit his lips. "I am."

"So," I start with a deep breath, "tour in under a month that needs finalizing. A wedding that, while out of my hands, needs to happen. And a bachelor party that needs to go down without blowing shit up."

He shakes his head as he takes a massive bite out of his burrito. "Yup" exits his full mouth as food falls out.

"Looks like we've got the makings for something here," I exhale my words.

"The makin's of what is the question," he says, chomping away.

I chuckle, sipping my drink. "Best man means best man responsibility. Any thoughts on the party?" I take a crunchy bite of a cheesy chip.

While we eat and start to think, I text Jeanine, asking to meet up with her later tonight. A strange request from someone who tried to make her go away for a big chunk of her childhood. She responds surprisingly quickly.

[Jeanine: Working on wedding plans for a while. What time did you want to meet?]

Of course she's working on wedding stuff. She's planning it in record time.

[Finn: Whenever works for you. 10? 11?]

An even more rapid response: I'm not liking how quick she's getting back to me. Something doesn't feel right.

[Jeanine: Sure. Sometime in there. Taps?]

[Finn: C U then.]

But here's the thing about this. I invited Jeanine out to tell her she can't be controlling. She's working with my schedule on this. She responded fast. Perhaps D.B. and the guys are just misinterpreting signals.

"Stripper or strippers?" D.B. asks.

With a raised brow, I respond, "Do you even need to ask?"

"Jeanine will never allow any of where this plan is already headed. She'll kill him if she knows he knows he's getting strippers at his bachelor party," D.B. realizes.

"Don't worry; Gregg won't know anything," I say while smiling a shit-eating grin.

"He still has to get married after this whole thing. You can't blow up the wedding because of some grudge against Jeanine," he scolds.

"I'm not going to," I defend. "But I'm also not going to walk on eggshells because of her either."

"Fine. We'll need food. And drinks," D.B. states the obvious.

"Done and done. I know a bakery that sells booze-filled cupcakes and booze-infused ice creams."

D.B. shakes his head at me. "You know places that others wish they knew. You sure we can do all this without blowing up the marriage?"

"Trust me. It will be a night to remember."

We enjoy our meal in a strange silence that only good friends can have. It's an unspoken understanding that our food needs tending to, as if by talking more, the food would not taste as good. So, we sit, enjoying the rest of our meal in silence.

D.B. finishes off the last bite, wiping his hands and mouth on a few napkins. "So, I saw Viv chattin' it up with someone new. You and her through already?"

I nod and search for a better answer, but it's hard to place words about twenty years of mistakes and yearning into a sentence or two.

He returns my nod after a moment. "I understand. Faith," he says.

"Yup" is all I can muster.

"We all have some version of Faith. The hand we couldn't quite hold onto long enough. Just slipped away like in the movies," he says.

"I got the comparison," I say, wiping my hands on a napkin.

"You and Viv seemed tight. She likes you. Or did. Whatever," he says, standing up to get a refill.

"It's all good, brother. Things happen. I gotta go talk with the bride-to-be now. See ya soon."

He bids me farewell with his two-fingered nodding salute and a wink.

On my drive to neutral ground for my meeting with Jeanine, I try to organize my thoughts. I attempt not to think about Faith and all the things I still have left to say. That's if she's even there—there's a small part of me that hopes she joins her sister. Another part, however, prays it's just Jeanine because then I can concentrate on the task at hand. I can help ease the tension the band is feeling over all this. I can also help her understand that a traditional wedding in three weeks' time isn't realistic for many reasons, but a ceremony and reception of a less-traditional sort may be feasible with just close friends and family. A nice chat is possible about how the guys worry about her becoming the proverbial Yoko.

But there's this larger part of me that hopes Faith is there. A piece of me wishes she tags along because she wants to see me; a part of her wants to be with me and that she rode with her sister to profess she was wrong. Maybe she doesn't want to throw away a second chance because of a rocky start, and that she is sitting there because she shouldn't have left things the way she did. But I know I'm not that lucky.

No matter now, though. I pull up to Taps & Corks to have my friendly-yet-professional business meeting with Jeanine and, behold, a sight for sore eyes. Sitting next to Jeanine, drinking a bottle of some craft IPA, is the tattooed, dark-haired raven that is Faith. The almost two decades after our first parting pales in comparison to the past two weeks, knowing that she is here, in Orlando, right down the road, yet still so far away.

I take a deep breath before exiting my car. I exhale, trying to push out all the nervous butterflies that still float through my insides every time I see her. I'll walk inside and say a friendly hello, no undertones of desperation or unconscious hinting at wanting to drag out our current demise. I step out of my car and shut the door. The sound of the door slamming shut as some guy stumbles out of the establishment grabs their attention, causing them to turn in my direction. They both raise their drinks in acknowledgment of my arrival. I see a friendly look in Faith's eyes, where she isn't staring at me with daggers waiting to pierce my heart. It's a nice start, but things can change. I see Jeanine, pointing in my direction and speaking a few words to Joe, the bartender, as I make my way to the door. He glances my way and nods as he begins pouring a Shanghai Tea. A drink on Jeanine is a gracious act from someone who spent a good portion of their younger years trying to drive me insane. Perhaps people do change.

I take a seat at the bar as Joe sets down my Shanghai Tea. I go to take a sip but end up drinking it all in one go. Perhaps I'm not as ready for this as I thought, or I just need a little help from this alcohol-infused friend.

"So, Mr. Fairlane," Jeanine starts, "I trust you've been good."

I try not to glance at Faith. I don't want to see the look in her eyes as she awaits my response. On the same note, I don't want to see if she's not looking or doesn't care at all. "Doing what I do. Which is why I'm here."

I see Faith nudge her body toward us while trying to act like she is watching the television and not listening. She polishes off her drink in the meantime.

I signal to Joe to whip us up another round and watch Faith as she glances in our direction for a moment, surveying the scene to make sure Jeanine and I are dealing no further damage to each other.

"And why exactly are you here?" Jeanine pries.

"The band is my business. Literally. Their future partly lies within my hands. Their business is my business. What affects them affects me. No one is mad here, but some people have some concerns about things," I say, watching Faith roll her eyes at me beating around the bush.

Jeanine twirls her hand, urging the point to come around. "What exactly is this thing that affects you and them that they aren't mad about but just concerned about?" She pauses for a moment. "Did I catch the drift of your vagueness?"

I laugh at myself because, as annoying as I find her, my respect grows for her with each encounter. I can understand why the guys want me to handle this and not them. She can be a little intimidating.

"Yeah, you did." Now it's my turn to pause because I don't want to blow up the band or her relationship with Gregg, but I don't know a gentle way to bring it up. "Five weeks is an unrealistic time frame to plan and execute a wedding. You only have three left. They will go by in the blink of an eye." "Execute" may not have been the best word choice.

I see Faith turn up the outer corner of her lip. A hint of a smile that sides with me, but who knows how far along she'll ride in my lane on this?

Jeanine straightens herself up in her seat, the words she's about to say dancing on the tip of her tongue. "I don't want him going on tour and forgetting about me at the first pair of tits to flash at his concert."

"Wow. First of all, why say yes to a man you think would forget about you over a pair of breasts? Secondly, Gregg's not that type of guy. He loves you and listens to you, which is the second point I need to talk about."

"What? That he listens to me?!" A proverbial defensive barrier erects around her in a flash. She is on full defense. "Like that's some bad thing to listen to your fiancé? Like I'm supposed to be nothing more than eye candy standing off to the side?"

I interrupt as I roll my eyes, "Easy there, killer. Not what I meant." I pause for a moment, hoping she will calm down.

"Then what do you mean?" she huffs out.

"I mean he's a talented musician with thoughts of his own, and some people feel that he's deferred all his judgment to yours," I say, downing the rest of my drink.

"So, I'm some fucking Yoko Ono now?" she fires back.

I take a long, obvious exhale, trying to calm myself and give myself a moment to think.

"Nooo," I say, rubbing my face. "I'm saying Gregg is a musician: delicate ego, not all that self-confident when it comes to the ladies, and, in this case, that's you. What I guess I'm saying is that he needs some reassurance from you that he can think on his own and that you don't hold it against him if he disagrees with your opinion."

"Couldn't have just led with that?" she says, with a small smile on her face.

"Not sure I could have. But now we have to address the first point." I signal for another Shanghai Tea.

"I want to be married, and I want to be married before the tour. In that, there's no leeway," she commands.

I nod my head. I have to think about how I'm going to respond because, again, I can't blow anything up. I can't point out the obvious: that the tour is only four months, and even that is a short amount of time to plan a wedding, or on a more existential note, marriage doesn't change anything in a relationship besides your surname.

"Okay, granted. But give me that the timeline is a little insane," I say, hoping to start a compromise of some sort.

"Yes, it is," she confirms. "But I have all the details figured out. All the big ones anyway."

"Like?"

"Colors for the wedding, besides white. Flowers for the tables. Officiant. DJ. Food. Open bar. Invitation design. Guest List. Rehearsal dinner and everything along with that. Even a list of about ten halls because of the short notice." She pauses with a smug, self-satisfied smile on her face. "Is that okay with you, or am I missing something?

"Time for guests to RSVP and make plans in their schedules to actually come to the wedding?" I retort in jest.

"Done," she says.

One word can sting sharp, but I'll play coy.

"I assume mine got lost in the mail?" I ask.

"No. Just assumed you'd be there. You are the band's go-to guy after all."

That settles that matter. And like that, the sting is gone. "Thank you. What about Gregg's input on the event?"

"We've been together long enough for me to know what he'd want. That way I can leave him to the band. I've been planning my wedding ever since I was a little girl. Everyone thinks about it. I just went a step further."

I see Faith nod her head as her sister speaks—her way of confirming what Jeanine is saying.

"I didn't realize you were that insane, but cool. It works," I kid.

I see Faith tighten her lips and tilt her head at my statement, a motion that says I didn't say the brightest thing just now.

"Not how to calm me down, Finn. There's nothing insane about wanting a great wedding. You only get one if you do it right."

"Wrong correlation, but I know what you mean," I say, not meaning to further stoke the fire.

"Wrong correlation?" she starts. "What the fuck does that mean?"

"I mean that you only get one wedding if you do the marriage right, not the wedding," I respond, hoping she backs off the point and gets back on track.

"Whatever," she snorts back. "I'll be married by the time the tour starts and everything will be better."

"Better?" I ask. I glance at Faith, who is shaking her head no to my question.

"Yes, better."

"Okkayy," I say. "So, three weeks and a wedding and tour finalization."

"Yup."

"You'll let him make his own decision and not hold a grudge if his opinion differs?"

"Yes."

"And you'll deal with the wedding stuff so he can do what he needs to with the band?"

"Sure."

"Sure?"

"Yes."

"All right."

"All right."

I turn to my new drink I have yet to pick up and polish it off in one take. "It's been a pleasure, ladies. Have an excellent night." I turn toward the door and begin to walk out. No begging or pleading in my eyes. No desperate tone in my voice. All business. All business and no Faith.

"C'est la vie," I whisper to myself as I open my car door.

"Wait," I hear Faith call out as she exits the bar. A sight for sore ears if there ever was one: a simple word to satiate my yearning for her to speak to me.

I turn to see her double time her steps toward me. I keep the door open but wait for her to reach me. While I do love the dance we do, I am a bit worn out tonight.

"I like the way you handled yourself in there," she starts. *Not a terrible way to start this off but where is she going?* I wonder. Is this a simple thank-you, then off for the night with her sister? Or is there more?

"Thanks. I had a little help from you," I admit.

"Saw my face a few times, did ya?" she laughs.

I return the laugh. "My mind still can't get over the fact she's not ten and trying to constantly ruin our, um, private time."

"She's grown and everything. Quite the spitfire when she's so inclined." Faith beams with pride and admiration for her little sister. Her sentiment brings a sparkle to her eye.

It is in this moment that I see why Faith was so unexcited for Gregg's proposal. Why she has the worry she does for her sister and that while, perhaps, no one can make Jeanine fully understand the future she has laid out for herself, I may be able to help shed a little more light on it.

But as quick as the sparkle is lit in Faith's eye, it has diminished. She jolts back to reality by the weight of the situation. Faith turns to her sister, who is laughing it up with the bartender as he says something to her, leaning in close.

"I'm not going to beg," Faith starts.

I want to say, "that's not your style," but she knows that, and I don't want to interrupt her either. I want her to keep her flow.

"But say something to her," she finishes.

I shut the door to my car. "What do you want me to say?"

I could point out the obvious; I owe Faith nothing, and that she broke things off with me, again. First, almost twenty years ago and again more recently. I could remind her that we are not an item, a couple, a force against the world. I am under no obligation to oblige her whims to protect her little sister, who, as I've learned, needs no protecting.

But then there's the other side of me. The side of me that will forever yearn for Faith, forever want to make her happy, want to see her smile. I know that my conflicting emotions are nothing new. My inability to take a side and stick with it will always be my downfall. But it's the hopeless romantic in me that idealizes what we could be. And it's that side of me that will always win.

She turns back to me, a sullenness in her eyes that screams please. A look that is begging me to do this for her because she knows I might be able to say something to her sister that will get through.

Damn me and my never-ending desire to see her smile.

"Anything," she says.

I nod and put up a finger for her to wait outside. I make my way back in and cop a squat next to Jeanine.

"Did we forget to discuss some other fun topic for the night?" Jeanine starts.

Joe the bartender sees me sit back down and before he even takes a step in my direction, I motion for another drink. What harm could it do?

"It's not all glitz and glamour," I say, starting with the obvious.

"Oh, God. Did Faith send you in here to give me some cautionary tale from inside the scene?" she says with a snicker.

"Nope," I say, taking a sip of my newly poured Shanghai Tea. "Just wants me to tell you something."

"So? What are you going to say?" she says, sipping her drink.

"I loved it. I wouldn't take it back for anything," I say looking out the window toward Faith. "But that's because she chose to leave me. Had it not ended, who knows where I'd be today."

Jeanine laughs. "So my sister sent you in here, in some last attempt to warn me of the road I'll be taking, and your warning is, 'You loved it'?!" She takes a drink and continues laughing. "How peachy."

"I loved the one-night stands and booze and drugs and fame and everything that came with it," I pause for a dramatic moment. "Because I had to love it all. You don't get the nights after a show goes off perfectly without the hangover and pain that comes the next morning. The angry boyfriends chasing you down the road with a baseball bat in some vain attempt to defend some cheating girl's honor. But that's not Gregg." I pause to take a sip from my tea.

I watch as the look of self-satisfaction and all-knowing starts to disappear from her face.

"I loved the mornings after when some girl I didn't know was staggering out from my bandmate's room in nothing but panties, rubbing the sleep and drugs out of her eyes, searching for the rest of her clothes scattered throughout the apartment or house or wherever we happened to sleep that night. Nights before those mornings were what the music is all about. But it's also about the overdosing and being there when it happens. It's about the downward spiral into addiction from not seeing anyone you love for months at a time. It's about the fights with bandmates because single-serving strangers night after night wears off and gets stale, and the bandmates are the only consistent sights, yet they drive you nuts. The inability to see the ones you love and, even in the day of Skype and Facetime and Snapchat, sometimes not seeing them for days or weeks at a time, because that's how busy life can get for people. And it's fun, and it's crazy, and it's maddening, and it kills, sometimes fast, but most of the time, it kills very slowly."

"So, what are you getting at, Finn?" she says, straight-faced as straight-faced gets.

"I'm saying Gregg is not like that. But he'll be around it every day he's away. I'm saying that even the happily ever afters in this industry are not nearly as happy as they are made out to be. And most are definitely not ever after. I'm saying this is the way things are, and you'll be on the sidelines while he's gone and that can be months at a time. It will be equally hard for you. Thoughts that you never thought you'd have will form in your head and will haunt you. You'll obsess over them and not know why. You'll rationalize the thoughts, and it will placate them for a while, but they will creep back in and will have grown and gotten worse. I'm saying Gregg is not like that. He's not like me. He's a good guy, and if you think everything I just laid out is okay, then Godspeed. That's what I wanted to say. Gregg's a good guy. But so was I at one point— at least I'd like to think so."

She sits there, barely breathing. I already see the thoughts forming in her mind. Now I have to wonder if I planted them there or if I was just the guy watering the seeds that were already sown, by Faith possibly. But they are there and sprouting.

"I'm saying he's a good guy, Jeanine. I'm saying he needs to be an active member of Spear Fist without you encroaching on that part of him. I'm saying this because it is my job to look out for the band, to look out for those I love. And while yes, you were the annoying little sister always trying to poke your nose where it didn't belong back then, you've grown into someone I respect. So that's it. That's how it is, and what you'll have to deal with. If it's starting to cause issues already, then you're in for a very long road, but Gregg's a good guy. He's not me, or at least not the version of me you remember."

I finish off my drink and salute Jeanine good night. I head out the door to an anxious, waiting Faith.

She waits at my car, pacing back and forth.

She hesitates with the nervous words she is trying to say. "What did you say?"

"The truth," I say. "It's what you wanted, isn't it?"

She nods and grabs my hand. Immediately, thoughts of a thousand different ways this could go start flooding my mind. But I try to quell the thoughts. This has not gone well for me in the past, and I am done getting my hopes up for someone who doesn't want me as I want her.

"Thank you. For talking. With her, with me. You don't owe me. But still, you do these things," she says, keeping eyes locked with mine. "It's these things that keep drawing me to you. These things that make me rethink everything."

"What are you getting at, Faith? I just said a few words to your sister. She proved herself to me. I respect that." I keep eyes locked with her all while trying to throw up a veil between us.

She lets go of my hands. "Finn, tomorrow night there's some of us meeting up at the restaurant. You should come."

That took a sudden and drastic turn. Did she see the veil and not what was underneath? Is she choosing to finally stop the dance we do so well, or is she slowing the tempo down a bit?

I smile because I want to say yes, but I've always said yes. I still want to succumb to my desire to be hers and her be mine. This time, though, I can say no, only because I have a prior engagement. This time it's not for a fan, or for a chance to get laid, or for some situation that will end badly. It's just to make a new friend and see a show.

"Thanks, I'll try to make it, but I'm heading to House of Blues to see a show."

Her eyes turn away from me. "Oh, that's cool. I mean, it was just a whatever. No worries if you can't."

"What is that?" I say, referencing her sudden tone change and verbal garbage. Is she suddenly shy about her feelings toward me?

"What's what?" She fails to be coy.

"The 'oh ... I mean.' Like you're asking me to a school dance, and I just said maybe."

"Nothing, Finn. Damn. I'm trying to be friends, civil, cordial, whatever since we're obviously going to be in close proximity for a while," she says, backing away a few feet.

"You left me," I remind her while opening the car door. "Again. I have plans. I'm not avoiding you. I'm not sidestepping anything. I have plans." I get in my car but leave the door open.

"Is this business tomorrow or a date?" She crosses her arms.

"Does it matter? You left me." I close the door and start up my car.

Faith steps up to my window, tapping on it. I push the button to lower the window.

"I don't want to be enemies." Her words are soft.

"We're not. But you wanted me to stop chasing you. You said that I hadn't changed enough. You said things, and these things all indicated for me to stop trying. So, for now at least, I am." I start driving off and watch Faith in the rearview as she stares at me. I can't tell if she's shocked I drove away or shocked I'm not trying to get her back.

I want her back. I do, but I'm not going to plead and beg. I spent too many years destroying good possibilities all at the thought of her. She's here now and has made it clear that she and I are not a thing. So why should I keep jeopardizing potentially good relationships for the off chance of her and me being an us? Besides that, tomorrow is just a thank-you for good CD recommendations.

CHAPTER 6

Speak of the Devil

T he start of this day is one that has become an all too unfortunate, common occurrence. A quick view of the news that plays out in the background as I eat breakfast tells of another school shooting, another group of kids dead. So goes life. I'm not overly left or right, but the sad fact is the people discussing gun control keep having the wrong conversations about it. Hell, I guess if I knew the proper discussions to have, I'd be in politics. But I can't help think that these kids don't even have a chance. I wonder how many of these kids being buried now even experienced a first kiss, a first love, first lay, or, hell, been in a fight. Seems unimportant now but without these small things, the bigger things like a first heartache or a first bloody nose from that first fight can't heal. It's in the healing that we grow stronger. However, it's the politics in between that kills these kids. What makes me

THE FORTUNATE *Finn Fairlane*

feel more than slightly selfish in this whole thing is that
I feel inspired to write.

Long Walk, Short Drink

No one's been perfect in history,
But some cross a line into insanity.
Tell us lies that become crystal clear
The thin veil that stops calamity.

Leading us down a ten-mile road
To three ounces of water.
Hundred and five and the sun beats down.
That's a long walk.
Leading us down away from our homes
To three ounces of water.
One o' five. Hell, we all might die
On a long walk for a short drink of water.

Feeding us bullshit they call steak dinner
Just to calm the masses.
We chew it all up and when we shit it all out,
They feed it to the lower classes.

Somethin' should go here, a line 'bout policy.
Somethin' 'bout the way we ship overseas.
Somethin' 'bout labor and cheatin' our own.
Somethin' 'bout jobs and bringin' them home.

Leading us down a ten-mile road
To where there used to be water.
Hundred and five, hell, we're all gonna die
On a long walk for a short drink of water.

Don't get me wrong; these lyrics may seem unrelated, but the point is still relevant. Living in Florida, there hasn't been a school shooting—yet. Who knows what the rest of 2017 will hold. I'm sure, though, that it'll come soon. We already had Pulse nightclub.

I can't let the daily news keep me down, not today. I have to find a way to relate it all to music, since that's what I do. A painter would take it out on a canvas. A novelist would write a book, and a screenwriter a screenplay. I make music. If art isn't a reflection of life, then what is it a reflection of?

After I finish writing the lyrics, it's time to make a few calls and book a few more tour stops. A task that doesn't take a terribly long time, and since I have some time before meeting Jacquelyn, I figured I'd call Faith, see if she's down for a quiet drink before she's surrounded by friends.

I find myself back, sitting at the day-of-the-week-fried-food-two-hundred-grams-of-fat-per-entree-over-priced-restaurant patio that not too long ago was our almost nightly haunt. While I wait for Faith, I feel a set of eyes staring at me. It's one of those things no one can explain, but when someone is staring at you, you feel it. The hairs on the back of your neck tingle. A voice inside your head silently warns you to look up and meet those eyes, which is what I do. I look up and see a heavyset lady in her fifties staring at me. The look on her face is anything but pleasant. I hate to use this term, but if she doesn't have resting bitch face, I don't think anyone does. But she sits, staring at me with her frizzy, sun-bleached hair in desperate need of attention, sunglasses resting on her head. I'm just sitting here with my drink, minding my own business while I wait for Faith, but here she is staring at me. Her judging, quadruple chin chastises me from afar. I smile at her, trying to disarm her razor-sharp stare, but she just snarls and shoves a whole mozzarella stick into her mouth.

As my level of feeling uncomfortable couldn't get worse, my savior arrives. Faith pulls up and gives a quick wave at me from inside her car, acknowledging my presence. I turn away from the bitter, middle-aged lady who stands up and walks in my direction.

Faith takes a seat as the lady stops at our table, eyes still trying to pierce me. "You don't remember me, do you?" she asks with squinted eyes.

From her words, I feel like we may have met before, and it went far worse for her than it did for me. "I'm sorry. I don't."

She nods her head and snorts a self-satisfying laugh. "Of course, you wouldn't! The famous Finn Fairlane, once too big to take the time for the little people. How's it feel to be one of us?!"

I look to Faith, whose look of confusion while shrugging and shaking her head almost makes me laugh.

"Look. I apologize for whatever I've done. I'm no saint, and sorry if you mistook me for one." My apology may be sincere, though I doubt she'll take it that way.

She looks away in disgust. "You left me and a line of people who'd been eagerly waiting hours to meet you. You just up and left with no reason why. You may have been famous once, but that time has passed. You acted like a grade A prick. I hope you're happy with yourself!"

She storms off after relieving years of repressed anger toward me. But she opened a floodgate of unpleasant memories, memories I wish weren't brought up tonight. The news from the start of my day is a foreboding of things to come.

But here's the thing of it: I sat and judged her moments earlier based on what some would call "resting bitch face." That's assuming I saw her before she saw me. Otherwise, she was giving me a dirty look. But I don't know her. Just as she judged me for all these years based on one action taken in bad timing, I judged her. How do I know she is not dealing with the loss of a loved one now like I was back then? If not a loved one lost, some tragic event that is causing her to take out her frustration on a stranger?

That's another thing in itself. People see a television star, screen queen, musician, whoever in real life, and think they have a solid understanding of that person based on a character they played, a song they misunderstood the lyrics to, or an interview or two they've watched on television or read in some magazine. But they do think they understand, so they approach and feel far more comfortable than the celebrity. And people will talk to you like you've known each other for years. Being on the other side of that, it's not always comfortable. It mostly is us thinking that we must pretend this stranger is a welcomed friend when all we really want is to be left to our own devices. But what happened, happened. Some lady I didn't sign a picture for years ago got mad at me today.

"What was that all about, Finn?" Faith asks in a state of confusion about the whole event.

"Something from a long time ago," I say, finally turning back to Faith. "Fun times, right?"

"Always an adventure with you," she says while laughing.

I just nod at her comment as I sit in awkward silence, my mind still lost in the memories the stranger resurfaced.

Faith watches me as I stare off into the vast distance. I can tell she's trying to read me, read my mind, but this incident she doesn't know about. She never heard because it was after we broke up. I kept it out of the news. But she tries to read my mind as she stretches her neck to reposition her head so she can stare into my eyes more comfortably. It is a welcome distraction from things long past.

"As fun as it is to sit here and watch you space out, I could be doing other things with my time," Faith semi-jokes.

I snap out of where my mind was taking me and come back to the moment with Faith, a smile on my face.

"Sorry. How have you been since…?" I let it trail off. She knows what instance I am talking about. "We didn't get much of a chance to talk standing in front of my car."

"Pretty good. Viv and I are becoming friends." I don't even need to hear the rest of her thought as she begins. I can feel that the rest of it will not end well for me, but on the other hand, if it doesn't end poorly for me, maybe it ends well for Faith or Viv, or both.

"She's quite the funny person," Faith continues. "I can see why you feel the way you do."

What the hell does that mean: "Feel the way you do"? I can sense her undertone. The subtlety of her fishing for me to confirm that she used the wrong tense: that my feelings are passed, gone, and dead. Why Faith needs such affirmation on this, I do not know. She's made her stance clear. Perhaps it's an "if Faith's alone, I should be alone too" thing.

"She's a good girl, but she saw too much of you when she looked into my eyes and not enough of her." I tell her that because it's honest. I don't expect Faith to run into my arms for some happily ever after moment, but if she needs solace, I can offer that.

Speak of the devil, and she shall appear. As if summoned from the "Finn doesn't need more crap today" section of my life, Viv enters through the swinging metal gate.

Faith turns as the door slams shut, acknowledging Viv with a head nod. Something about this moment actually seems a bit more relaxed than the last time we three were sitting on this patio.

"I know you don't have too terribly long," Faith says, turning back to me. "So, I told her to come early. Sitting alone on a restaurant patio can give off the wrong impression."

Viv grabs a chair next to Faith. "Finn," Viv says in a direct and almost unfriendly manner. The smile on her face contradicts her tone.

I return her greeting in the same manner, which causes her smile to widen. She does have a sweet, beautiful smile. Her snake bites beautifully accent it. I find it ironic and slightly amusing that here the three of us sit again, though this time on better terms.

There is another strange, extended moment or two of awkward silence. Three grown adults sit in this uncomfortableness of knowing each other and each other's recent pasts. It's this silence of not knowing what to say but not wanting to engage in small talk about the weather because small talk would seem petty. So, Faith and I sit, sipping our drinks, while Viv just kind of watches us, adding to the uneasiness of the moment.

After what seems like an hour of silence, but was probably more like forty-five seconds, I decide to stop the junior-high charade. "Drinks?" I ask.

A unison "yes please" from both ladies sends me inside for refreshments. I stand at the bar, waiting for my drinks, while a bartender who looks like he belongs in a dads-only rockabilly band pours them for me. No visible tattoos or piercings but he's got the pompadour, chops, sly smile, and softer-sided rockabilly attitude, and he seems kind enough. I turn around and watch through the windows as the two women I love are sitting on the patio, side by side, engaging in some sort of conversation and, judging by their faces, a pleasant one too.

I find strange happiness standing at the bar, watching them talk. Faith seems happy, or at least not weighed down by anything at the moment. There's a part of me that is at peace watching her. Faith laughs at something Viv says. A smile crosses both of their faces. For a second, it makes Faith look like a mischievous cherub. She used to be my mischievous cherub.

The clink of the drinks being set down behind me is my cue to pay the barkeep and return to the world outside. I toss him a ten spot for his efforts. He thanks me with a two-fingered salute against his downward tilted head as he nods and winks. Very befitting of him. I'd expect no other sort of thank-you.

I head back out to the uncomfortable silence, but that time has passed. Instead, I am greeted not by a "Thanks for the drinks," but a "What's her name?" by Viv.

I set down the drinks, completely confused by the question.

"The bartender was a dude, and I didn't ask," I say, turning back to look again at the bartender. "At least I'm pretty sure that's a guy."

Both Faith and Viv laugh at my expense. "No, no, no," Viv clarifies. "The girl you are seeing tonight."

Now that I know the direction of the question, I can feel that no matter the answer, my balls shall be busted on.

"I see you two were laughing at my expense while I was inside." I sample my drink.

"Actually, Finn," Faith starts, "laughing at the poor girl about to be sucked into the loving disaster that is you."

"Thanks," I say as dryly as I can but somehow still sound far more sincere than I intended. "What makes you think I'm seeing a girl tonight?"

"Your vagueness about the whole thing, for one. Like you have to hide your life from me." Faith pretends she's all hunky dory.

"Well, it wasn't too long ago it seemed I should have, even though I tried not to. And by too long ago, I mean..." I defend.

"I know what you mean. Things can change in a few weeks-time, Finn," Viv chimes in.

"Yeah," Faith confirms. "Look at the two of us all buddy-buddy when a month ago, we didn't know you were banging both of us."

"What the hell are you doing? It was at that same time you were banging me back and still with Ronnie. We don't owe each other anything like that. And you, Viv..." I let myself trail off because, with her, I don't really have a leg to stand on.

The ladies both stare at me, waiting to finish my thought on Viv. "I'm sorry. I didn't realize that things were where they were." I should have realized that after her roommate Izzy walked in ready for a three-way, but Viv's eyes told me she didn't want one. Maybe she just wasn't in the mood. Maybe I read too much into it. Perhaps a part of me knew what I was doing and wanted to blow things up. I could list a hundred different reasons or justifications why I did what I did. Excuses and hindsight reasoning don't matter now. Now, all that matters is I made presumptions and ended up here.

"Relax, Finn." Faith jumps in while lighting up a smoke. "We're all good," she says, gesturing to the three of us. But in my experience, anytime anyone uses the phrase, "We're all good," it usually means that, in fact, things are not all good.

"I'm glad the three of us are on such good terms." I gulp down the rest of my drink. "That's relieving. But now I must be off."

"So soon?" Viv asks. "Everyone should be here shortly."

I shrug and point to my imaginary watch. "Show starts soon. I'll be by afterward, I think."

Viv feigns a playful pout. "See you soon, Finn."

"You too, Viv." I turn to Faith, whose silence has been noticeable the past few moments. "You okay, love?"

She looks in my direction but stares past me, lost in thought. Something is simmering beneath the surface. It's a look I've seen on her many times, so I know I just need to wait a moment for her to find her words.

"I'll walk you to your car." She has found some words.

A silent walk to my car finds me leaning against a closed driver's door as we stare at each other. She forces out small, quick smiles of regret.

"You know I've never stopped loving you, Finn. I tried to convince myself otherwise, but it never worked," she says, now staring at the ground. "I don't know why I'm saying this or what I expect from you in return. I just thought … it just felt like it was something I needed to say."

"I know." I lift her chin up. "Tonight, it's just a show. I'll come back afterward if it's not too late."

I lean in and give her a hug. We look at each other with the same regret-filled eyes we've stared at countless times past. Our lips hold their position less than an inch apart, begging to touch each other, wanting to feel their warmth smushing against one another. She smiles, then plants a proper kiss on me. Nothing in her kiss is deep or passionate in a way that lends itself to us ending up on the blacktop next to my car, grinding on each other. Her kiss feels like she's telling me I'll always be her number one, but now is not the time. There's no other way to describe it, and if you've ever been privy to either of the above, you know, without a doubt, you've felt it and which one you've felt. If you've ever felt both kisses, then first, you don't need an explanation. And second, my condolences on having felt that tinge of pain. If you have never felt either, the feeling is further ineffable. The latter kiss is filled with so many emotions, all ready to boil over … if only the timing was better, but no physical sensations can accompany its description.

She walks away, back to Viv, who I see shaking her head. I smile a half-smile, knowing that after all these years, Faith and I still drive each other crazy. I grin not because I enjoy driving her crazy but because no one can drive you that insane without equally feeling that much love for them.

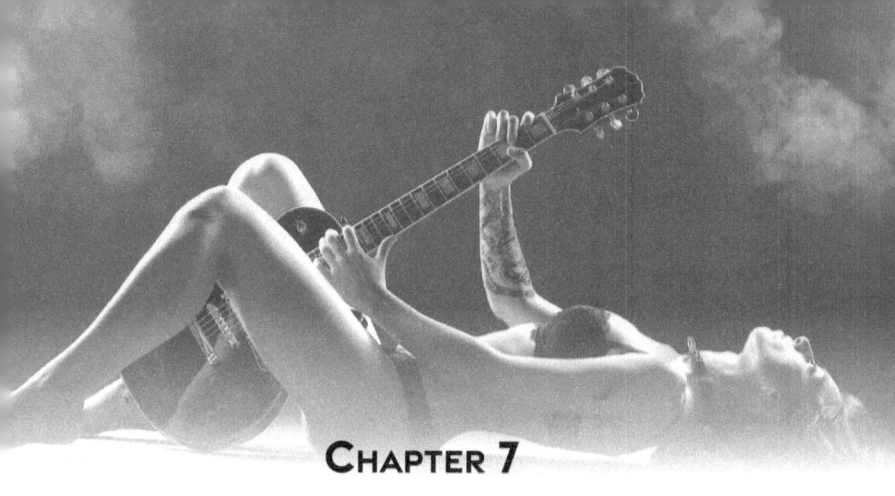

CHAPTER 7

Take the Time

After getting through security, I stand right outside the lobby to House of Blues, looking around for Jacquelyn. After a small flood of people pass by and clear, I see at the other end the bitter, middle-aged woman who had finally gotten her chance to let me know how she felt all those years ago, bringing back once more a flood of memories I wish I didn't have.

My old band was doing a record signing at Empire Records or Tower Records or some such place in Bloomingdale, Illinois, or some suburb around there. We had all our tables out and set up. Our new release, Tweaker, was overflowing in the display setup, waiting to be purchased by many enthusiastic teens and adults. We had our piles of Sharpies® at the ready to sign copy after copy and guitar after guitar. The crowd outside had grown immensely and had been waiting for who-knows how long. The store employees were laughing with us over some stupid joke, and everyone was happy. It was set to be a great day for everyone.

Then my phone rang. The caller ID lit up, letting me know my mother was ringing me. I sent it to voicemail, figuring I'd call her back the next day or whatever. But it rang again. Again, I sent it to voicemail. She dialed one more time. This time I picked it up.

She sounded hysterical. From the moment I said "hello," all I heard were tears. I stepped away from the table to a quieter spot in the store. Through her tears, she told me how my childhood best friend, Marty, and his family, had been in an accident. I could only make out every few words. They had been friends of my family for years. We'd spent holidays together, a few vacations, weekend excursions, etc. We drifted apart here and there but were always close. It was one of those relationships that no matter how long it had been, once you were together, it seemed like it was yesterday we were together. Now I was listening to the tears of a grieving woman tell me about a drunk driver, a crushed car, a flipped car, a lamp post, a semi-truck, all four something, but I was able to gather the gist of what she couldn't say distinctly. The next, unintelligible word was not one I wanted to hear.

All I knew was that a whole family was gone. Three generations of blood lay mixing together on a highway somewhere off 294 near Chicago. It was a moment that gets ingrained in your mind. A moment that forever will be painted crystal clear, like when Kennedy was shot or when the Twin Towers fell. It was a moment of disbelief so intense that all reality was pushed aside, as my mind tried to rationalize how this was and could not be.

But in the end, it was. I had to be there. I had to meet up with my family to see their family one last time. I turned to the rest of my band. They saw the look on my face, and the color was gone. I was pale; I know it because of how nauseous I felt. My stomach churned and tried to keep down my lunch. All I wanted to do was get there, get to where I needed to be, to be with them, with family. But I had to run to the bathroom. And, of course, in true record store fashion, the bathrooms were anything but sparkling. I knelt onto a sticky floor, under a flickering light, onto something that I could only imagine was a combination of unrinsed floor cleaner and drying urine. I didn't care. I started heaving and vomiting into a toilet that had even grosser brown and red stuff caked onto the rim under the seat. I couldn't stop. My body was trying anything to make it not real, anything it could to deal with the news. But it was real.

I don't remember how long I was in the bathroom. At some point, I remember leaving out the back door and the band telling me they'd take care of the rest. But I was their front man. I was supposed to be there, signing away and making music fans giddy at the excitement of meeting me and getting my autograph. Instead, I was on my way to say a final goodbye to a family that was my family.

The drive to the hospital was numb. I was in a trance, trying to play out the scene in my head and how it happened: how a person could drink so much, they no longer cared about the safety of others; how a person could drink so much that they no longer think they can't safely operate a vehicle. I tried not to imagine what the moment was like. Did Marty and his family see the accident approaching? If so, did anyone try to warn the driver? Were they blind-sided? Did they feel the impact, or was there no pain? Did they die on impact? Then the worst possible thought on this situation hit me. What if Marty or his wife or his mother didn't die on impact and watched help-lessly as the rest of their family bled out, as their own blood drained from their bodies as car after car drove past, apathetic to their distress? I tried to shut my thoughts down and not think about the accident. I decided to concentrate on driving so I could make it there safely, so that I wasn't the cause of someone else's loss of life.

By the time I arrived, the rest of my family was there. The room I was taken to, just past the emer-gency room entrance, had its door closed. I remember the nurse who had handled the situation since the others arrived leading me to the room and stopping outside the closed door. She turned to me and put her hand on the door. She didn't turn the knob but asked me if I was ready. I could hear the others in the room crying. The sounds of their pain and loss muted through two inches of wood. It was real, and I had to face it. I nodded my head. She turned the handle. My mother was inside sobbing as my father stood with silent, stoic tears streaming down his face. There were gurneys lined up next to each other: one each for Marty, his wife, his child, and his mother. So much loss in one room. I just stood there. I couldn't *cry. I couldn't feel anything to cry for. I was trying to rationalize it or block it from hurting again. Stop it from being real.*

To see tubes sticking out of a child's mouth from resuscitation attempts, same with his wife; their lifeless bodies still begged for help, silently calling out to be saved. I remember they didn't look dead. They looked like they were asleep or lying in wait to yell, "Got ya." I didn't see injuries. Their faces had scratches on them. Otherwise, they all still looked like themselves. I couldn't wrap my head around it. I was told they died from crush injuries. His wife and child died more slowly from internal bleeding than he or his mother did. Their deaths were far quicker, near instantaneous. I found little solace in hearing those words about them.

Death is still death. It's why we scream into microphones. It's why poets take a pen to paper. It's why oil and acrylic get brushed and thrown onto canvas. It's our way of trying to grasp the concept and deal with the loss, a demon in our lives we must find peace with. I thought I had found peace with this event until it decided to rear its ugly head in the form of a bitter, middle-aged woman who ripped those old wounds wide open again, twice in a night.

So, I'm forced to sit and stew in the memories of the faithful departed. A crowd of people walks by me as I stand in my thoughts just outside the House of Blues, but the commotion of the present event flings me forward in that fateful night.

A rush of first responders poured into the emer-gency room as a man who knelt on the gurney did chest compressions, one after another, until they halted and got the man intubated. I looked at the man on ventilation. Some nurse saw me staring through the curtains of Marty's room as they all passed by, talking over the patient's body.

"They had to use the jaws of life…" The rest of the sentence was lost on me. I didn't know this guy. He didn't know me. But I saw him clinging to life, struggling to hold on. I wouldn't have remembered the man, except for the next thing that my ears picked up was implanted in my mind forever. "He was the driver who caused the crash."

At that moment, all compassion left my body as it was replaced by a deluge of hate and vengeance. Here was a guy who couldn't stop at a couple of drinks, a guy whose lack of self-awareness, lack of self-control just cost four people their lives. I did not care for this man and, had I not had more self-control, would have made sure his life ended right then and there. But I knew it wouldn't bring them back. I knew that my desire to serve vigilante justice would only make my life harder than it would be without my friends we called family.

So, I watched as his life teetered. Each time his heart rate changed on the monitor, my eyes grew wide with hope that the numbers would fall and drop to zero. I hoped that the defibrillators would do no good, just zap away at his remains. I hated myself for feeling those emotions. I hated myself at that moment for wanting one more life to end that night, as if it would be some sort of cosmic balancing to even the score. Except you can't even a score like that. Yes, *he was at fault. Yes, his actions had consequences, dire consequences. Had he lived, he would have had to live with those consequences, but he didn't.*

After an hour or so of sitting with my deceased friend and his family, I watched as the drunk driver's heart rate shot up to over 200 beats per minute and then dropped to zero. Flatline. Something in the crash caused a strain on some heart vessel. It perforated, causing him to bleed out internally. I don't know if he felt any of the pain that my friends felt. I don't know if that matters. There was no cosmic scorecard. There was no karma to balance there. The only thing there was death. And a lot of it.

The crowd disperses, pulling me from my memory, leaving the angry, middle-aged woman to see me. Snarling like some feral dog, she walks up to the threshold of the inside and outside. No re-entry, so at least she can't touch me. She squints at me, ready to say some anger-filled jab to make this day more downtrodden.

I speak first; I don't need more from this lady. "Listen, I don't know why you held onto that sort of anger for all these years. It's not becoming on you or anyone. If you think my life was or is something close to perfect that you must knock me down a peg, then I'd suggest looking in the mirror to see what's really bothering you. I'm sorry I had to leave that night. I didn't want to and wish the events that made me duck out didn't happen. But they did, and I'm sorrier than you will ever know. Now please, let go of the anger and try to enjoy the show."

She stands there, mouth agape and motion-less, dumbstruck as to what she can say next. So, I turn around and look back into the Disney Springs grounds for Jacquelyn.

CHAPTER 8

Galactic Brain

There Jacquelyn is, passing through security and picking up her belongings from the tray, dressed to the nines for the occasion in a strategically torn midriff top that came from somewhere between the late 1980s and early 1990s, executed with a bit of both side and under-boob showing. But she has the carefree attitude and confidence to pull it off without it looking like an attention grab. Just someone who is comfortable in her own skin. Her hair is pulled back into a ponytail so loose, it's a wonder it is still held back, with perfectly executed video vamp makeup to finish the look.

She strides over to me, stopping less than a foot away, and hands me my ticket to get inside.

"Nice jacket." She puckers her lips in some half playful, half sensual way, grabbing my sports blazer that is downplayed by my T-shirt and torn jeans.

"Just a style I like. Love your outfit. Very throwback," I say with a smirk.

She grabs my shirt and pulls me in for a quick, surprise kiss. My eyes widen from the blitzkrieg, and I look down at her eyes as she locks lips with mine. She too is staring up at me and finishes her kiss with a smile.

"Now that that's outta the way, wanna buy a girl a drink?" she says, prancing off to the bar.

The shock of her kiss and the boldness of her actions leaves me dumbfounded for a moment. She looks at me with a tilted head, surprised that I was, well, surprised.

"Cat got your tongue?" she says while laughing, gesturing for me to follow her.

"How do I know you don't have the herp or some-thin'?" I spew off the first thought that comes to mind.

"How do I know you don't? Now, come on!" She sets off to the bar at the opposite end from the venue entrance.

I shake my head to bring myself back to the moment and follow her. After ordering a couple of whiskeys on the rocks, I turn to her.

"Thank you for all those recommendations. I'm really digging them, especially Flatfoot 56." She smiles, looking out over the crowd.

"No problem," I respond. "Do you always thank strange men by taking them to concerts?"

She shakes her head while drinking her whiskey. "Not usually. I just like to have fun. Be in the moment, ya know?"

I nod because there's something about her, something I can't quite place my finger on. I watch her turn out to the crowd on the floor. She's watching them as I watch them. She's looking for those people who aren't just here for a few beers and a night out. She's looking around to see whose life needs some musical therapy.

I was curious. I didn't read any marquee on the way in. I didn't see the ticket she handed me but just pocketed it. I pull it out to see who shall be gracing the stage tonight—Nirvanna: A tribute to Nirvana. Interesting. We shall see how it goes.

I was going to ask if she was even a Nirvana fan, but she's staring out at a father and his pre-teen daughter standing in what will surely become the mosh pit. Not far off from them, next to the security railing against the stage, I see a tiny woman dressed like she's straight out of a nineties street-workout video but was probably born in 1993. She yells at some shaggy-haired guy who hovers at least a foot taller than her. He stands there frustrated but, judging by his sloped shoulders and defeated posture, is used to the abuse she's doling out. While I can read lips a little, she's talking at him so fast I can't get much. I do read out a "You don't own me" phrase, to which he replies something that elicits an eye roll from her.

Jacquelyn and I watch this go on for a few more moments before he storms off in our direction. Poor guy: who knows why she was so mean just now or why he stands by, taking it. The evident frustration on his face signals this is not a new occurrence. He stops at the bar a few feet from us and orders two beers and a double shot. The bartender puts down the shot first, and the abused boyfriend shoots it before the bartender can say, "Here ya go." It's that kind of night for him.

We stand at the bar there watching more of the crowd for a while. Stagehands set the stage with banners that indicate a Blink 182 cover band will be up first: fun times of corporate, pop-punk with an easy-to-digest flavor for the masses. It's everything that Nirvana was not, but three-quarters of this crowd is too young to know the difference. The sign of my times goes forward in reverse. Most of these kids think the two bands come from the same mental place. Rebellion, outsiders trying to find their voice—Nirvana, yes. They were on the forefront and helped create a genre that spoke to so many. The other band just played fun, punky music for teenage girls to lose their virginity to. But whatever, I have a new friend standing next to me.

"I wouldn't have taken you for a people-watcher," I say, leaning into her so she can hear me over the blaring house speakers.

"I am," she says, shaking her head as she continues looking out toward the crowd. "My job doesn't really allow for much watching."

"What do you do, Jacquelyn?" I ask, hoping to learn something about her.

"Nothing important," she evades. I let it go. "What do you do, Finn?"

"Drink a lot and make things happen."

She stops watching the crowd and turns to me. "I see how it goes. I avoid, so you avoid. This could be fun."

A guy closer to my age stops next to me at the bar. He orders a few beers and turns to me. His face lights up like he's seeing Santa Claus in person. He grabs a pen and coaster off the bar and takes a step to me.

"Dude. Bro! Holy shit!" he starts off. Yes, I've heard those four words in that order a few times before. At least he's friendly. "This is so awesome!" he continues as he looks around for a familiar face to show me off to.

I look at Jaquelyn, who's suddenly very interested in why this guy is geeking out over me.

I grab the coaster and pen. "What's your name?"

"Ben. Ben! My name is Ben!" He starts shaking with excitement.

It's been a while since someone got this excited to see me. I look at Ben. "Think we can keep it between us?" I whisper in his ear, while signing the coaster with a personalization.

He nods his head with such vigor I am afraid he may herniate a disc. Then, he walks off, pocketing the coaster, a 360-turn-around in coolness.

"What was that all about?" Jacquelyn asks with a raised eyebrow.

"Nothing. Just thought I was someone else."

She shakes her head in utter disbelief of my excuse but lets it drop for the moment.

The house lights dim as the show starts. The flashing red and blue lights from above the stage make their figure eights as the Blink tribute band goes through the usual suspects of radio hits. The crowd eats it up. I must admit it is a relatively entertaining show. I just never understood the allure of pop punk outside of the catchy hooks. Or is that it? Escapism in its most capitalistic form. Just something for the masses to eat up and consume so someone else can profit off their struggles? But now, for the moment at least, I know why I am here. I watch Jacquelyn bob her head to the tunes as she sings along, escaping from whatever hell has a hold on her during the daylight. There's a part of me that wishes I could be like them. Just bobbing along to the music, but pop punk had always felt so empty to me. I need more from it. I need to be a part of it, part of its creation, part of its exhibition. Even here as I watch her, I can't get into it. Maybe I am just angry that I can't be one of them, so easily able to escape their problems in this music. Maybe.

Maybe I am just not a fan.

Either way, Jacquelyn looks good. She seems happy with a smile on her face as she urges me to sing along. I want to sing along. I want to be happy, but all I can think about is the woman I left behind tonight to be with this one, this woman who knows less than Viv did when she and I first met. Jacquelyn doesn't even know who I once was. Perhaps what I find so appealing about her is that she thinks I am just a regular guy. I smile at her as she gets me to sing a line or two about how it ain't so and how I won't go.

The show goes on and on. I try to enjoy the quiet moments with this enigma of a girl, who apparently just wanted someone by her side tonight. But the Blink 182 tribute band exits the stage, causing the house music to come on the speakers. The house lights get a little brighter. If she wants to talk to me, she has some time. And it looks like she does.

"Having fun there, big guy?" She watches me look around.

I turn to her and smile. "Yeah. Fun show."

She scrunches her face, not really believing my words. She looks me up and down, searching for an answer written on me somewhere. She stops at my hands, which are hanging out my pockets by the thumbs.

She leans into me. "What's her name?"

I keep close to her but turn to her ear. "No her."

"Not anymore, huh?" She grabs my left hand, examining my ring finger for a sign of a long-worn ring recently taken off. "Maybe. Maybe not." She puts my hand down. "I'm smarter at these things than you'd think."

"Perhaps." I grab her hand in turn. "I don't see a ring on your finger either."

"God no. Did that once. Not happening again." She twists her face in disgust of the thought of marriage.

"You're what? Twenty-five? Divorced or widowed?" I pry.

"Kinda personal there, Finn, don't ya think?"

"A bit, but no more than your presumptions. Turnabout is fair play." I let slip a smile, hoping it lightens the mood.

Jacquelyn nods in agreement, smiling back. It's funny because on stage are two pretty decent-looking ladies in cheerleader uniforms straight out of a Nirvana video, entertaining the crowd and I couldn't care less. This is partly because both of the cheerleaders have a look on their faces and body language that cry out desperately for some sort of narcotic/upper fix, but mostly because Jacquelyn has me intrigued.

"I'll answer if you'll answer why that guy geeked out back there," she asks.

I think hard about it for a moment while I purse my lips in thought. "How about we enjoy the show?"

She nods and turns back to watch the sedated cheerleaders lead on. She leans into me and wraps my arms around her. It feels nice but also friendly. I wonder what it means. I'm not clinging to some notion that this may lead to sex or the love I've been waiting for all my life or some trite thought. I mean, I'm just thinking about if she is interested in more or feeling her way around those parts, or just a touchy-feely kinda friend with no intentions of anything more. I don't try anything. I don't let my hands wander. I refrain from whispering sweet nothings into her ear, not that I was tempted to do such things. I just try to enjoy this night as much as I am able to, relax, and take in anything that happens to me.

I look around at the crowd as the house lights lower once again and three guys dressed precisely like Nirvana, down to the iconic white sunglasses and bleached hair with overgrown roots, take the stage. It's like reliving the days gone by of discovering grunge music and the religious experience that went along with feeling the music on a spiritual level. I see it happening again. I look around and see a bunch of kids, some still high school-aged, mesmerized by the music pouring off the stage. Even Jacquelyn has relaxed a bit in my arms because she likes to sing along to all their pretty songs.

I am enjoying this night out, away from my life in music while being surrounded by it. This evening is a nice break from the norm without straying far from it, but there's a thought running through my head. *What will I tell Faith when she inevitably asks about tonight?* It doesn't mean anything more than this moment: a new friend is resting in my arms. On the same note, if she wasn't a "she" and just some new guy I friended, I wouldn't be doing this, but she already got past the first kiss and she didn't seem impressed. So, what will I tell Faith? What is there to say to Faith? Not much, I suppose. But then again, how do I feel about this whole thing? At the moment, I don't know, and I don't really care. I'll deal with whatever may be brewing in the back of my subconscious when I need to deal with it, a proverbial bridge I will cross once I get there.

Right now, I need a drink.

I pull my arms out from around her and whisper in her ear, "Gonna grab a drink. Want one?"

She turns around. "I'll come with."

I start through the crowd of people standing shoulder to shoulder. Jacquelyn grabs hold of my jacket, so she doesn't get separated. We bob and weave our way to the bar. Once again, I see the shaggy-haired guy who was earlier accosted by the pint-sized woman. His mood doesn't seem to have improved. It makes me wonder why someone would stay in a relationship like that, what someone could see, or think they see, in someone else that lets their own self-worth be sacrificed.

The same bartender from earlier sees us and makes a circular motion with his finger at us, asking if

THE FORTUNATE *Finn Fairlane*

we need another round. Impressive that in a crowd of well over a thousand he remembers us; a talent that lands him a ten spot for himself.

Jacquelyn gets close to me, if only to speak. "You keep looking around."

My focus turns to her. "It's what I do. I people-watch."

She shakes her head. "Naw, I people-watch. You're looking for something."

"I don't know," I answer because I really don't. I look around at everyone, everywhere I go. It's a habit I picked up after Faith first broke things off back in 2001. Maybe I'm always looking for her.

"Well, whatever you are looking for, I hope you find it. You seem very intense and yet very laid-back at the same time."

My focus shoots to her to look her in the eye. "You do know those are contradicting descriptors?"

"Exactly. But that's you. You need to relax and listen to the world," Jacquelyn says, shouting at me over the music. "Stop looking around. You can't see the details when you keep looking at the big picture. You need to listen to what the world is telling you. Even in a loud place like this, you can hear it, if you listen."

She might be right. Who knows? I think after my start down here, I'm still in the mindset of trying to fit into the lifeline of the city, intertwine myself in some way. What I fail to realize is that after what I've been through down here, after the people I've met and involved myself with, I am intertwined. I am in the city's lifeblood.

The rest of the show is spent with us at the bar side. We aren't drinking a ton, one or two with waters to make sure we stay soberish, but we found our spot here. We found a place where we both feel relaxed and enjoy the show for what it is.

As the masses exit and make their way back to their cars after the show, I swim with the current, so to speak. We first stop at Jacquelyn's car. I seem to be doing a lot of standing outside vehicles lately. Maybe it's just a thing that happens in clusters, like celebrities dying in groups of three. But, either way, here we stand, outside her bright yellow BMW. I notice a few key marks running along the driver's side of her car. I run my finger along them as if I am inspecting them for some microscopic clue.

"I gotta get that fixed." She waves off the key marks.

"Lover's quarrel?"

She lets out a hearty, throated laugh. "Ha! No. Just some guy who wishes we were lovers. Some men just don't understand boundaries."

I take a step back, not that I was even that close to her at the moment. She notices and smiles at the gesture.

"You're safe. If you weren't, you'd know it. However, if you were hoping for an invite back to my place..." She trails off.

I shake my head. "Oh no," I start with a dog-sly smile. "I actually was hoping for an invite to the back seat. Figured the theme of the concert and all."

She gives my arm a quick jab. "How about a good-night kiss where we stand?"

I nod my head as she moves closer to me. "I like that."

She rises on her tiptoes as I lean my head down a bit. Our lips get close to each other. We hover for a moment as if some unknown chemical reaction may occur if our lips met. This time is different from the first, surprise kiss. For a moment, she hesitates as our lips gently caress. I can hear her breathing slow down, but there is a nervous quiver to her that, after tonight, I would not have expected.

I pull away for a moment and look her in the eyes. Her carefree look has changed. Her face no longer reads of the woman I met earlier. There's a vulnerability in her eyes that is new to me. From the shakiness in her breath, it might be new to her as well.

"You have done this before. At least once. I know you have," Jacquelyn says, looking into my eyes. The corners of her lips begin to pull upward.

I move in and lock lips with hers. The feel of Jacquelyn's well-moisturized lips as they press against mine sends a shiver down my spine. Our kiss starts slow and not too shallow but grows into a deeper, more passionate kiss. Our lips move in sync, and our tongues dance around.

The first time you kiss someone, starting with your very first kiss at some young, tender age, and leading to your latest kiss outside a car reliving the glory days of grunge, a million thoughts fly through your head, and all in about the ten seconds it takes to lead up to a first kiss. *Are we going to connect? Is she a closed-mouth kisser? Will she use tongue? Too much or too little? Will I use too much tongue for her? Will our rhythms match? Do I have bad breath? Will she have bad breath?* And about ten thousand other questions fly through your mind, hoping you can make all the necessary adjustments before she cuts the kiss short and bids you goodnight. But all those thoughts, all those worries disappear the moment your lips connect. The instant you are finally in the moment, everything falls away—if the kiss is magic. And the good thing about most winter nights in Orlando is they can still be warm with the enchantment from those summer nights. And if her thoughts are similar to mine, there's magic right here.

She pulls away from me, biting her bottom lip. "Mr. Fairlane," she playfully bats her eyelashes, "that was ... thank you."

"Thanks is all mine." I pull at my shirt collar, cooling myself off. "I think now is the perfect time to go our separate ways for the night."

Her face scrunches a little, as if she's holding back either a smile or tears. "Is this it then?"

"Only for the night," I say, realizing that I just sounded either really romantic or like a stalker.

She opens the door to her car and takes a seat. A shiftiness in her movements has surfaced in the moments since we just kissed. Perhaps I am not the lip-locker I once was. Did I do something to make her uncomfortable? That would not at all be my intention, but if she took something I said in jest as a serious statement, then I may have ruined potential. Making off-color remarks is never my intention.

"See you soon, Finn." She shifts her car into drive and starts to idle forward. I shut her door and watch her drive off.

I stand for a moment and make sure she's okay as she drives away. I'm not really sure what happened at the end there, but something changed. Something shifted in her. I can only help but think that I did something to somehow ruin what was a great evening. My evening, however, is not over. Now I must return to the woman for whom I will always be a slave.

My drive back to the patio section to see Faith, and whoever else might be lingering there, wasn't long; still, it gave me time to think. And think I did, about what this night could mean or could have meant, what I could have done or said to have suddenly put her on edge. Maybe it wasn't something I said or did. Perhaps it was her, but if it was her, then there was nothing I can do about it and nothing I can change. I can only control what I do. So, I ponder what I did, what I said to have possibly caused the sudden shift, but I come up empty, which means I wait a few days to give her time to cool off and hope she returns my call.

But with those thoughts aside, I can turn back to the task at hand: the balancing of the fragile relationship I have with Faith and not doing anything to screw that up any further.

I pull into the back side of the restaurant and park my car. As I approach the hedgerow where I first explored anatomy with Viv, I see a rustling in the trees. I laugh to myself to think that not too long ago, it was myself and Viv back there reliving our pasts' moments of innocence lost. I must have laughed a little too loudly as I hear hushed whispers and a pants zipper. I slow my walk a little to see who it might be that will be doing the same walk of shame back to the patio that Viv and I once did.

A moment later, out from the bushes, pink-and-black hair peeks out and I laugh as the head attached to that hair is Logan. She stops, frozen by the sight of me, as a shit-eating grin crosses her face. I smile and nod at her accomplishment of the night. This makes me wonder that since she's into innies, not outies, who it might have been that ducked behind the foliage with her. Here's the thing I've learned in life though: never wonder a question you aren't prepared to hear the answer to because when the answer is spoken, it's there and you can't unhear it or unsee it. I see Logan reach back into the bush and grab a hand. The body that follows the hand is one I recognize. One I care for. One I was behind those same bushes with a few months back — Viv.

Except now I am Faith and Ronnie rolled into one, both proud of Logan for living her life and scratching an itch that obviously needed scratching, but also hurt because this is someone I care for and somehow, even though it was me back there with her, disappointed she would sully the place that was ours. Though in all realistic thought and reasoning, that place was probably hers and a few others' before it was ours, but it still hurts. Maybe sting is a better descriptor. But any words that I may use here, it's strange to be on the other end of the scene this time.

Logan takes a few steps toward the patio when she realizes that Viv and I are eye-locked with each other, unsure of what to say. Logan stops and turns toward me, quickly reading my face. She sees a palpable awkwardness in the situation but can't quite place her finger on it.

I try to be polite about it as Viv and I owe each other nothing. Well, at the very least, she owes me nothing. But what do I say? At least it's not a cup of male tears? That's just barbaric and dumb, but then the fact that that specific thought popped into my mind makes me wonder, when Ronnie saw her and I pop out from the bushes, if he too had once been behind them with her. Regardless, I'm not going to say that. So, what will I say to break the awkwardness of the silence among us?

"Good times," Viv says to break the silence as she walks toward me.

"Indeed." A laugh escapes me. "I see you know Logan."

"You know him, Vivian?" Logan interjects, extending a pointed finger my way. "Do you know who this guy is?"

"Yeah, babe. We're friends. Met a few months ago," Viv says, calming Logan down. Viv turns to me and says, "Logan and I used to date. Reconnected when D.B. invited her out tonight."

"I take it he's here then?"

Viv nods her head.

"Hey! Wait a minute!" Logan's excitement is uncontainable. "So you're in charge of Spear Fist?"

I scrunch my face and tilt my head side to side. "I wouldn't say 'in charge.'" Yes, I just used air quotes. "Just providing a guiding light for them in their current tour. Did you get my email?"

She shakes her head. "I didn't think... I was going... Sorry I didn't get back yet."

"Calm down. It's all right. I see D.B. took me up on my advice to contact you so here we all are."

Viv looks at me with a look in her I have felt on my own face before. She's waiting for the other shoe to drop in this situation. "You okay, Finn?" she asks.

"D.B. mentioned you started seeing someone." I nod my head at Logan for verification.

She shakes her head. "That was nothing. A short-lived mistake."

"Shorter than me?" I try to make a joke.

She forces a smile. "Yeah. Nothing to waste more thought on. So? You okay?"

I smile and look up to the night sky full of stars. I inhale a deep breath and let it out before looking back to her. "Perfect. Come on."

I am perfect though. As much as it stung moments ago, the sting is now gone. It feels like the waters have calmed down and things are somehow falling into place, at least for the moment.

We all take a seat next to each other on the patio, and as if no time has passed, D.B. is surrounded by a small crowd of people hanging onto his every word. Vincent and Neil strum their hollow body guitars to an acoustic version of Slipknot's "Snuff." Per expectations, there are three girls all ooh-ing and aah-ing over the musicianship of the two. The rest of the patio is filled with familiar faces laughing and enjoying the warm night and cooling breeze.

The one face I don't see outside is Faith. I look around as if I may have passed over her and not noticed, but she is not there. I peer through the windows to the bar and see her in there staring out at me, a smile on her face. She points at me, then pantomimes a drink. I nod yes and wink. She salutes me and turns back to the bartender.

D.B. excuses the current conversation that has the surrounding crowd entranced and turns to me with an extended fist that must be bumped. So, I do. Our fists explode back as we make explosion noises ... cause that's how we roll.

"What's the word, good sir?" I ask after our fists settle down.

"Making friends," he says, nodding to Logan.

"So, this will work then?" I ask, tossing a glance to both D.B. and Logan.

D.B. nods with a wink as Logan shakes her head with enough enthusiasm for everyone—an answer I assume is yes but is actually everywhere in between, to which I nod back. "Good to hear." I turn to Logan. "You need to decide how long you want to be on tour together. That's something I can't decide. Only you, your guys, and Spear Fist can."

She nods back to show she understands but doesn't say anything. "Any luck in finding that new member?" I ask.

She snickers at my use of the word member. "After I met you, I did my research into you and decided to make a few calls and such."

"And?"

"I have a few leads," she imps out her words.

"This tour is much bigger than anything you've been on before. Leads won't cut it, and the tour launches in under a month. Make something happen and soon." My words come out like a lecturing father, but the need calls for it. If she wants to take her band farther, now is the time.

Throughout this whole exchange, I can't help but notice that Viv has been silent and staring at me the entire time. I'm sure something akin to guilt has been haunting her, taunting her, or tugging at her since our eyes met as she emerged from behind the trees. I figure I need to soothe whatever it is that irks her.

"Viv, you all right?" I start.

She nods her head, though the look on face says otherwise.

"Just making sure. Your quiet is kinda creeping me out," I joke.

She laughs, relaxing her face. "Been a long couple of days."

I see Faith say something to her sister and Gregg before walking out with a couple of drinks. She seems to be in a much better state of mind than before I left for the Nirvanna show.

Faith hands me my drink and says she'll be back in a moment. She steps away to a familiar face who I've never talked to before. They have a few laughs, making her settle down on the arm of the patio couch. I smile and turn back to my group.

"Strippers?" I say to D.B.

"Strippers? For the tour? That could be fun," he says, obviously not keeping up with my random thoughts.

"For the bachelor party. Gregg's inside so we can talk, no?" I ask.

"Yeah, we can talk," D.B. confirms. "And it sounds good to me. I can always have a few extra good-looking ladies around."

"What else are you planning? Strippers are fun and all, but you'll need more," Viv offers her unsolicited input.

"Did you ... want to go?" I hesitate.

"I mean, I'm not his closest friend, but we are friends. Plus, a cause for celebration is a cause to celebrate. So … yeah," she says, then quickly adding, "if that's cool."

"Yeah, that's cool," I chuckle. "Logan, I know your chosen preference, and since you'll most likely be touring with the band, you can join us if you'd like."

"Ass and titties, hell yeah!" she says with the excitement of a twelve-year-old boy who's never seen either before.

"So then, Viv, what else do you think we need for the party? Isn't the point of a bachelor party to get drunk in some hotel room with a stripper or two doing unmentionable things to you that you'll never speak of again?" I ask, sipping my drink.

Lighting up a cigarette, Viv offers further thoughts. "An event. Something other than sitting in a strip club, or hotel room, shoving ones and fives into G-strings."

"Like what? Stripper paintball or something?" I try to figure out how to fit strippers into another kind of event.

"I'm with Finn," D.B. interjects his thoughts. "Bachelor parties are about boobs and booze, baby! I've never been to one that wasn't."

"Straight-up strippers is just so passé. You gotta do more. Like maybe a road rally or something, then strippers," Viv mentions, straight out of the early nineties.

"A road rally? Like a scavenger hunt in a car?" I attempt to clarify.

"Yeah, sure. Something other than a strip club. Unless that's what you want is just booze and boobs," Viv finalizes.

"Wait. Wait," D.B. says, waving his leather wrist-banded hands. "What's the end goal of the road rally?"

"The strippers, duh," Viv starts. "You don't tell him anything about what you have in store for the night. You start the road rally doing offbeat findings. Like a G-string for a guitar instead of the underwear. Stuff like that."

"Oo! Oo!" Logan interrupts, the proverbial lightbulb above her head lighting up. "Then in the middle of the rally, you stop off for a steak dinner. Something with a pink center. Or a side of chicken breast!"

I laugh out loud at Logan's excitement over a bachelor party for a guy she met only earlier tonight. She has the same look on her face as she did when I saw her decide to buy the microphone at George's Music. I can see why Viv used to date her and, as they put it, reconnected tonight.

"A road rally might be cool, but it will have to be epic." I set that conversation aside. "That bit of planning aside for the moment, how's the night looking, D.B.?"

"Same ol' same ol,' my man. Just waxing intellectual about the existential," he says, chugging the rest of his beer.

I lean back in my seat, nursing the drink Faith had bought for me. I zone out of the conversation that continues around me as I focus on Faith. She's still sitting on the arm of the plastic wicker patio furniture, talking with that same girl she settled in with after handing me my drink. I want to go say something to her, not to bother her or start anything but just to say hello, though I don't want to interrupt the conversation she looks so content with carrying on. I sit back, watch her, and listen to the ambient noise that surrounds me on this patio. I feel the light, cool breeze pass over my face and neck, and I can feel every little hair blow in it, every inch of my skin cooling off in the night. I feel very comfortable just sitting, a hard situation for me to feel comfortable in.

I don't go say anything to Faith, as she is happy. I don't want to be overbearing, though something in her conversation has her look my way. She stops talking as she sees me. She raises her drink to me in a silent toast and takes a sip. I watch her as she stands up and pats her friend on the shoulder before walking back to me.

She doesn't stop at me though. No. As she passes, she motions with one finger and an upturned hand for me to follow her. I excuse myself from our current conversation and head out of the patio. I follow Faith around the corner to the trees, but she doesn't go behind them. She stops at her car parked in front of them.

"We could go behind the trees and make out a bit?" Faith jests.

There's something in that joke, though, that is both sad and true. The tone in Faith's voice is a bit sullen and desperate, not desperate in a pathetic way but in a "Please don't say yes to this" way. This is all fine and dandy because I am not going to. Going behind trees isn't characteristic of Faith, and I've been there before. That's not something I wish to relive with Faith as my substitute for Viv.

"What's on your mind, love?" I say, keeping a close distance but being careful not to touch her. I want to. I want to grab her tight and run away, hand in hand, like some stupid fairy tale but it's not what she wants.

She turns her stare to the ground like some shy high-schooler asking a boy out for the first time. We've been there, we've played that part, so I can't understand why she's playing it again.

"How was your date?" And there it is, the million-dollar question of the night.

"I'm here. Aren't I?" I take my finger and lift her head. She nods in adolescent-like, guilty admittance of agreement. "It was a thank-you, not a date." At least I think that's true. I could be wrong, but I'm sure I'm not.

"Is everything all right at work? Do you need money or something?" I am still confused as to why we walked back here.

She pushes back from me a little bit. "No," she huffs out. "Everything is fine. I just thought … I don't know what I thought. Maybe I wanted to go make out behind the trees. Maybe I wanted some company back here." Her voice takes a drastic turn to sarcastic. "I thought you might want to hit this." She pulls an already packed glass bowl out of her cigarette box, a lovely blue-and-green, blown glass piece with resin built up to give it a tie-dye look.

I let the subject of what's on her mind drop for the moment, as whatever it truly was has disappeared. So, we sit smoking a little weed away from the rest of the company.

The smoke circles around us as we exhale, dancing in the thoughts we both want to say, though we sit silently for a moment as we partake. I can feel the tension build as she wants me to say something. I just have no idea what it is she wants me to tell me, which gives me no ideas of what to say. We sit, passing the bowl back and forth, letting the THC mellow out our minds and relax our souls.

I look up to the night sky and see what stars I can see through the pollution of the streetlights and buildings surrounding us. Faith leans into me as I look up. I wrap my arm around her and pull her hair back behind her ear with the other hand. She, too, looks up to the sky to try and steal my sights.

"Is she cute?" Faith continues staring skyward.

"Cute? Like a five-year-old? No," I respond.

"Not like a five-year-old. Cute as in, would you do her?" Faith asks straight-out.

"That's a strangely inappropriate question." I shift my gaze down to her.

She pulls away and faces me. "God, you already did, didn't you?"

Not the most relaxing weed she's ever smoked; either that or if this is relaxed for her, she needs to unwind some more.

"No, we didn't. She did kiss me though. But I think she did it more out of curiosity than anything else." I pull Faith back in toward me, but she resists. I stop.

"What the hell does that mean? Out of curiosity?" She takes a deep breath. "Damn it, Finn. Whatever. You don't owe me anything."

I nod. "I don't, but you asked. I'll always tell. I think she just wanted to see if it would be any good or if I had something on my mind. Like she wanted to get the awkwardness out of the way so we could both enjoy the show."

I look into her eyes as I speak because I want her to know. I want her to know that other women will always be nothing compared to her. I will always put Faith first. That is something she needs to know.

"Why?" She scrunches her eyes.

"Why what?"

"Why tell me? Why still carry a flame for me after all these years? Why hold me up to some standard that is impossible? Why all of it?"

There you go. The world around me has stopped spinning. All guitars in my mind have stopped playing. The feedback from the amplifiers screeches out the deafening, high-pitched timbre. The cymbals ring out as everything around silences. The music has died as I have been asked the impossible question. I must now try to answer what I could not answer for the past nearly two decades in song. I must now try and find a way to verbalize feelings that have controlled and guided virtually every action I've taken since the day we split, if not since the day we first had margaritas. But what can I say? What is there to say that hasn't been said before? What words are there to summarize in a few sentences everything I have done over the last 6,205 days of my life? Which, for all you *Rent* fans, is 8,935,200 minutes. I only know this because Katy—of Katy and Patrick—had me watch that movie and that song stuck with me in a weird way. So, I calculate the years from time to time. Strange, I know, but back to the moment.

The thing is I want to answer. I want to tell her how I feel: how I've always felt; why I've always felt that way; how my feelings aren't just about my idealization of what a relationship should be. Tell her that my emotions are not about my Magical Kingdom-addled brain thinking a prince has a right to kiss a sleeping stranger, and everything will be happily ever after. I have no false conceptions about relationships; that is not where my feelings for this woman lie. My feelings lie in everything she does, everything she says to me, that has ever made me feel like more of a man than I should feel like or would have otherwise.

My feelings are about her and how she treats others. They are about the amazing woman she was back then that pushed me to become something more. They are about this fantastic human being that wants to better herself so she can perhaps help someone else in her own way, right now, and for the past decade, has been through boosting confidence with a great cut or color. That's what cosmetologists do, but when she does it, it puts a smile on her face as well. I know this does because I know her. I see the way she cares for her sister and doesn't want to see her end up in her shoes in ten years. The fierce loyalty. All these things I can say about her and why I love her.

But here's the catch. These things that make someone fall in love with another person—they are moments in time, instances that happen without much notice or fanfare, but I noticed. I saw what happened and why they happened. I can't sit here with her, both of us flying high, and cite examples from her life that are the reasons I fell for her. To state all the individual times over the years I can remember that added to the overall feeling—call it love, call it what you will—would sound like a stalker guy watching her from up in a tree. But the years that made her so endearing to me were so long ago. Yes, since we've been back in each other's lives, I've seen those moments, which is why I know she hasn't changed. Perhaps I am holding onto the past, and there is no present or future. Maybe I am wrong, but to operate under such assumptions would make for a life full of hesitation, and that is not fun. Rock 'n roll isn't about thinking about sex, wanting to try drugs, and almost putting on a record. No, it's about doing all these things and doing them to the fullest.

I look Faith in the eye. "I can't answer that in this state of mind. It wouldn't do my words any justice. It wouldn't be fair to you to hear them coming from me while I'm not totally sober. But I will tell you. Just not at this moment."

"Finn..." she starts, but I pull her in and plant my lips on hers.

I do this because she needs to know I love her. She needs to understand my feelings. My advance is not uninvited. She reciprocates my move, and our lips dance like soft waves of the ocean crashing on the shore. Our tongues swim in each other's mouths, ever searching for the meaning of life. Our eyes are closed, as I think about all the time I have to make up for, all the time I have missed and the things she has been doing. How I want to hear about them; I want to hear about everything. I want to be there for her, but I can't make grand gestures. We have to take it one day at a time, one moment to the next.

I gently place my hands around her waist and hold her. I feel her body pressed against mine. I know what lies under her clothes and how amazingly beautiful it all is. Now is not the time for that. That moment must wait. Now is all about the kiss, a kiss to rival any kiss throughout the ages, a long-awaited hello that says we both made it; we are both here.

She pulls away, and as I open my eyes, I see her eyes slowly open. An ear-to-ear smile on her face. "Ronnie called me. He wants to work things out."

And my newly found cloud nine has dissipated. I am free falling to the earth below with no parachute, no safety net; only the hard ground below to stop me. My body feels like it is spinning in a free fall, no control over anything. I am just waiting for my demise.

"Just being honest about things?" I am now very confused about the moments prior.

"Tryin'." She is looking everywhere but at me.

"Was this a final kiss? One final way to say 'I love you' but please move on? Or a welcome home of some sort?" I say, bobbing my head around to try and catch her attention.

"I don't know what I am going to do. It's not that easy to turn your back on five years," Faith says with a frown.

"I can wait. It's what I've done for seventeen years," I say, her eyes finally reconnecting with mine. "Is that why you wanted to get together earlier tonight? To tell me this?"

"I didn't get the chance. Finn, this isn't easy, ya know?" She looks me dead in the eye. I don't flinch. I don't want to flinch. I don't want this moment to end. I don't know if I'll ever get a moment like this again. Looking at our history, past and current, it is likely I am, but if I were to assume I would and never do, then I would hate myself for cutting short this moment. If we do get to do this again, then this is just another beautiful memory I will have.

"But I thought you said he wasn't the one. Or that he wasn't right. What you told me before." The desperation in my voice is subtle but there. I can feel it creeping in and slowly taking over.

"I know what I said. But he's a good guy, Finn."

"Strapping, young lad if ever there was. Great punch too. But you don't need someone to tend to you like a pet. So, do tell." I was able to hold at bay my never-ending desperation for her until the last three, little words.

She caught it too. She looks on for a moment, watching my face, my eyes, my mouth, every inch of me for something. What she's looking for I do not know, perhaps the answer to life or another kiss goodnight. "Finn. I don't know. I love you both, and it's hard to let go of either history. Of either past. I don't want to. I just need time."

She turns away from me and gets in her car. I watch, unable to move, as my body is unable to gain control of the free fall and smacks against the blacktop below. But, since I'm not actually free-falling 20,000 feet, I live. The pain in my heart swells. I can't move to not watch her drive away. Perhaps had I been able to answer her question, she would have stayed. If I had given her whatever sign she was looking for while searching my face, maybe she wouldn't have left. But she did, and I am once again alone.

Chapter 9

Light Me Up

Fuck inspiration. Fuck the tour schedule and planning. Fuck it all. It's not that I want to be angry; I just am right now. There's a feeling deep inside my mind that nothing I am doing is right or will be right; that everything I'm doing will all be for nothing, and it tears me up to think like that sometimes. This isn't the first time I've been caught in these thoughts, and the sad truth is it probably won't be the last time, but right now I have nothing. I don't have the girl I've been thinking about for all these years. I don't even have the new girl who has added to my confusion for the other girl. I have myself. I have the money I've made. I have my toys. However, none of those last two things provide any sort of consolation over not having the girls.

Once you start this line of thinking, it's hard to leave, not because you want to stay wallowing in this self-pity or whatever it might be. No, no one actually enjoys wallowing in self-pity; it does nothing to better yourself. What makes it hard to leave is that once one lousy thing creeps into your mind, it opens the door for every bad thing, big and little, that has been patient and quiet, waiting in your subconscious, to race to the front of your mind. Every little fight you had where you said something you came to regret or did something that wasn't becoming of you, every time you spoke in a volume that became hostile, is fresh in your mind again.

Every. Little. Thing.

It just sits right behind your eyes, playing over and over like commercial ads reminding you of everything that you were and still might be. The frustration from the reminders only angers you more because you know you aren't that person. You are better than you were and even when those things happened, you weren't proud. But you can't take back what you said and can't undo what you did.

Maybe it's my thinking that's flawed. Perhaps it's me. All I know is that right now, nothing feels right. Nothing feels real, and all I have to help me feel better is a six string and whiskey. One of those things is a long way to the bottom. I don't want to drive down that road again.

The fact is, though, as angry as I am right now, and as much as I feel unproductive and want to watch the world burn for a moment, I'm getting places lined up. Maybe productivity even when it stems from negativity is still good. At the very least, it's still productivity.

It's been a few days since Faith told me she was going to try and work things out with Ronnie. I know it's only a matter of time until that blows up again, but

I don't have the power to move things along for them. I accidentally did that once, and it hurt … my face. I don't dare think about how much it would hurt if the situation somehow repeated itself. Not that it would. In the past few days, I've taken care of a lot of the tour arrangements for the following months, and things are looking good. From hotels and motels to even the no-tells that we'll be staying at and the venues they'll be rocking are almost all lined up. Once I start making one phone call, the rest just seems to happen. The label is doing radio ads for the local region and poster ads for the farther reaches of their fandom and to draw in new ones.

But that's just it: this is what my life has been for so many years, and it feels empty. I want to share it with someone who is as excited about it as I once was. Someone who can breathe life back into me and make me feel like I have meaning and purpose. Wouldn't that be a great cosmic joke? We're all full of piss and vinegar about life until we find our purpose. Then it becomes dull and unfulfilling, repeating itself over and over, draining the life and will to live out of us until we die. *The Grand Irony of Life*. Album title of the moment right there.

There's a part of me that hates thinking like this, a piece of me that knows I am being petulant and unreasonable, a part of me that knows I have friends that would take a bat to somebody if I asked them to. But even those friends are only my friends because of the industry and what I've done for them. So yes, I feel alone, and there's a part of me that knows I may have done this to myself. There's another part of me that wonders if everything I'm feeling right now is just stress-induced anxiety. Will it all calm down after the wedding and after the start of the tour, or will it continue until I can find someone who doesn't care about the material things I can offer them and wants to be around me for love of the game? For love of being around me?

I am almost forty and still struggling with feelings of inadequacy and inferiority since as far back as I can remember. The sad thing is, even when I point out to myself, or someone points out to me, all the things I have accomplished in my short stay on this planet, all I can do is listen and sing along to "Bohemian Rhapsody" playing on my iTunes, about how anyone can see that nothing actually matters and nothing matters to me.

But on the other hand, I know what I do matters, maybe not in the cosmic sense spanning galaxies and clusters but it matters here, on Earth. On this rock we call home, what I do matters. People listen, and they are affected. And that is something. But of all the people I may or may not have changed with my music, how come I can't find something to affect me like that? Or is that the missing muse I'm now once again lacking in my life? Damn, I hate this feeling. I want it to go away.

The fates answer my cry to the universe with a text message, a simple sign that things may not be as bad as I feel they are right now. Jacquelyn apparently is the sign I was looking for, as her text reads,

[Jacquelyn: You around?]

Short, simple, to the point. The point though is what I don't get. I know this isn't a booty call. Booty call? Is that phrase even alive anymore? No matter though, it's not that.

[Finn: Yeah. What's up?]

I reply, not wanting to come across like an excited puppy waiting for his new home.

[Jacquelyn: Wanna come over? I'm off work tonight.]

I don't really need to think about it. Yes. Yes, I will go over. I take a moment to text back. Not that I needed it, but I didn't want to respond too quickly. I am relishing in the fact the universe listens sometimes.

[Finn: Sure. I'll need your address.]

I grab my wallet and keys and head to the liquor store. I figure a nice bottle of whiskey since it's what she drank at the show. She might like more than whiskey, but I don't want to bring something she doesn't like. Thing is, I don't know what she wants, of course besides hanging out. Maybe she doesn't have an agenda, just looking for a friend. What could be more friendly than a friend with whiskey? I don't want to seem like I'm asking her to go steady with me by bringing a bottle that's too nice, so I figure I'll just grab some Gentlemen Jack©—quality enough to not get sick but not expensive enough to give mixed messages. Maybe it's just whiskey; I shouldn't over-think it.

As I pull into a parking space for the liquor store, Jacquelyn texts her address and tells me to bring a swimsuit. I'm already out, so I figure I won't swim. At least now I feel like she's inviting me over when there are going to be other people. I mean, who invites one

person over to go swimming? That just seems a bit …
I don't know … strange.

I make my way through the light traffic on I-4 and
end up at her house a short time later. As I pull up, I
realize I either missed the life of a short party, or she
has other things in mind. I'm about to find out which.

"Those don't look like swim trunks," she says,
opening the door.

"Didn't get the message till I was at the store buying
this," I respond by holding up the Gentleman Jack.

"It's cool." She smiles, grabbing the bottle. "We
don't need suits anyway."

The mystery that is Jacquelyn confounds me each
time we meet, but it's not a bad thing. Seeing her
brings a sense of calm to my otherwise chaotic mind,
a sense of peace that only Faith used to bring but now
only adds to. I look around the otherwise empty house,
scanning for signs of life besides her and me. I see
nothing and hear no one.

"Who all is coming by?" I ask, following her to the
back lanai.

She looks back at me for a second while she continues walking. "In case you can't tell, I don't have
many friends."

"I find it hard to believe that someone like you
doesn't make friends easily," I say, trying to be smooth.

She opens the sliding door leading to the pool,
sectioned off from prying eyes by a privacy fence. "It's
not that people don't want to be my friend. Don't make
that mistake. I'm just selective. Too many people want
to be friends with me for the wrong reasons."

I chuckle because I can understand her sentiment. There are moments when the single-serving stranger by my side is nice, but it's not real. It never is. The connection isn't with me; it's with what I do, but I don't know what she does. The elusive being that is Jacquelyn hasn't told me what it is she does, but I can gather it is something that doesn't yield many close friends. Given her looks, I bet she's a model. I chuckle, and that causes her to turn back to me.

"What's so funny?" she asks, dipping in her toes to test the waters of her hot tub.

"I can relate," I mutter, looking around her pool. The in-ground hot tub spills over into the long pool, whose circumference waves along the sides. The pool lights within the waters change color every ten or so seconds, adding to the allure of the evening. Next to the hot tub is a wine glass with old wine stains at the bottom—a sure sign of nights spent alone in contemplation about something she'll never tell.

"I'll be right back," she says as she disappears back into her house, still carrying the bottle of Gentleman Jack©.

I wonder what it is she wants tonight. A friend to hang out with or someone to help her forget something? Whatever it is, I am not going to overthink this. I'll enjoy it for what it is, and much like the Nirvanna concert, listen to what the universe is trying to tell me.

I slip off my shoes and socks while she is inside. I carefully test the waters on the first step into the hot tub. Hot, but not scalding, a gentle heat to complement the chill air tonight. From behind me, I hear the door slide open and the clink of two glasses against a bottle. I turn back around to see a bottle of Cabernet Sauvignon and two glasses in one hand and two towels in the other.

"About the other night," she says, setting the glasses and towels down on a table next to the pool.

"No worries," I interrupt. "You don't have to explain yourself to me." I do find it interesting I bring over Jack and she pulls out a Cab. Maybe she plans on me coming back. Perhaps she just wanted wine.

She gives me a half-smile of appreciation for the interjected words. She pops open the wine and pours a glass for each of us.

"I'm glad you came by. It's hard to find good people when you work in an industry where they have the wrong idea about you based on what it is you do." She hands me my glass. That was a long-winded response, if ever there was one.

"My objective tonight is not to find out what you do for a living," I say, raising my glass. "To new friends."

She clinks my glass and takes a sip while keeping her eyes locked with mine. "So, you didn't bring a suit?"

I shake my head, eyes still locked with hers.

"We're adults here, right?" she says, looking to the hot tub.

"It would appear so," I reply with a curious mind.

"Since you don't have a suit, neither will I." She takes off her top.

And in about the most confusing three seconds of my life, I try unsuccessfully not to stare at either the most perfect set of God-given D cups ever grown or the most natural-looking fake boobs ever. I don't want to be staring like some high school boy at his biology teacher that he's lucky enough to finally nail against the classroom blackboard, but I am. Not even so much in the fact that she just so nonchalantly took off her top, but the fact that she did it without the implication that this is going anywhere.

She sees me staring and smiles. "Eyes up here, big guy."

I snap out of it and nod in agreement with her words. "Yeah, yeah, of course. Yeah. Didn't mean to."

She turns around and starts unbuttoning her shorts. "It's just flesh, my good sir. We all have it."

And there it is: no more thinking that Jacquelyn is some mystical, mysterious, mythical creature. Oh my. No. She is just someone comfortable in her own skin and sees no reason to be modest about it.

She grabs her glass of wine off the table and slips comfortably down into the hot tub. She takes a sip and waves the glass at me. I know she is wanting me to take off my clothes, but I freeze. It's not like this is even the first time I've gone full monty in a hot tub. It's just my first time with her. The thing about this moment isn't that a female wants me to get naked. It isn't even that an attractive woman wants me to get naked. The notion that nags at my brain, making me feel like a redheaded mermaid falling for a guy who doesn't know she exists, is that I do feel something for her. It's the ambiguity of my feelings for her that makes this moment so nerve-wracking. I know I can't place it precisely, and that inability to do so is causing me to freeze.

"Scared there, champ?" she calls me out. "Or ya gonna get in?"

I snap out of my brain fog and come back to the moment. "Yeah, I'm coming. Just a little chilly." I set down my glass of wine and start to unzip my jeans. She lets out a "bow-chika-bow-wow" like cheap music from bad porn.

I kick off my shoes toward the table; one hits a leg of a chair, jarring the awkward moment into a little more awkwardness.

"Did that on purpose," I say, trying to play coy.

"Sure ya did." She laughs, calling my bluff.

I take off my top and fling it over a chair back. The cool air of the night sends shivers down my spine and goosebumps form across my chest. Sure, I shiver a bit from the cold, but more so from the nervousness of the moment. I know I must get down to what God gave me, but the sudden cold breeze is doing nothing to help my cause with the little man, my special guy who is getting smaller and smaller with each passing second. So, I drop my jeans and take one leg out, but as I go to take off the other pant leg, I stumble a bit on the damp concrete. A few fumbled steps, and I grab a patio chair. The chair is so lightweight that it slides with the leverage from my body, sending me to the cold ground.

She claps her hands while saying, "Bravo! I give it a seven out of ten."

I look up from the ground and smile through my wounded pride. Standing back up, I know this is the last step before there is nothing between Jacquelyn and me. This is the final moment that separates men from MEN.

I drop my drawers, having no shame left after the fall. Maybe it's the pride that has abandoned me. Maybe it's that I'm standing here buck naked, and my little man looks like a turtle who's retreated into his shell. Either way, I drop them. I stand before this gorgeous woman in nothing but my birthday suit.

"Well, hop on in. The water's nice and hot."

I start to step down into the hot tub, the temperature of which might be able to slow boil an egg, but it feels so nice against the cool air of the night. As I take another step down, my whole body starts warming up. I sense the heat of the water climb my legs and radiate throughout my entire torso and down my arms. My red-eared slider starts coming out of his shell.

"Your wine," she says, gesturing behind me.

I turn around, having forgotten my glass from the moments caught in my head. I grab my drink and return to the waters. I sink down opposite her. As I settle in, I watch her as she looks around the night sky to the stars above. The ambient color of our surroundings changes with the underwater light in the pool, as it cycles through deep red, blue, green, and white, and back again, over and over. The wavy lines that shape the pool add a sense of calm to the evening.

"I find it hard to believe that you have no one else you'd rather be with tonight," I say, calling her bluff.

"Believe what you will, Finn. I like the time I've spent with you so far. Figured I'd see what you're like just hanging out." She sips her wine, then continues looking to the skies above.

I relax some more and slide down in the tub till my neck and head are the only things above water.

"It's amazing what you can find on people when you search their name online." She brings her gaze to meet mine.

"Some more than others, I presume," I say, sipping my Cabernet.

"The real question is why do you want to hang out with me? There must be someone else you'd rather be with?" she says. She starts to creep her way toward me.

I could be honest. I could just blurt out that I'm here because I'm momentarily angry at my life choices and back in college, I should have stayed with the girl I was with. I should have made the conscious decision not to be an asshat. I could tell her that I am here because the woman I want to be in this hot tub with is working things out with her current guy; that this girl that Jacquelyn has never met is trying to erase the image of me being balls deep in her from her man's mind. But let's be honest, that would not exactly be the nice thing to do. So, a comforting spin on the truth it is.

"I too choose my company wisely. Someone as selective as you must understand." I pretend not to notice her inching my direction. I look around her backyard at the chaise lounges under an umbrella and the small, round four-seater table with painted PVC chairs next to the loungers. I scan my way around the flower garden with what I assume is an attempt to grow some kind of foliage.

She stops about halfway to me, reaching out to grab the bottle of Cabernet, refilling her glass. She doesn't inch closer after setting it down. The thought that maybe she was just slowly going in for a refill does occur to me, but the pacing of it seems a bit peculiar.

"I've read some interesting things about you, sir. May I inquire if they are true?" She asks her question in a tone of voice that is both very straightforward and not lacking politeness. The question to me shows that she has not had any real run-ins with anyone who ever once was, or still is, famous. Bringing up particulars of one's past is sort of an unspoken taboo, but there is also an innocence to her question that makes me think perhaps she's just making conversation. I mean, I haven't heard her phone buzz or ring at all tonight. Maybe she isn't one who has a cornucopia of friends waiting to get shwasty at a moment's notice.

"If you read it, it must be true," I say, smirking. "Otherwise, why would it have been said?" I start inching my way to her. I figure it seems to be the thing to do, so why not do it? She doesn't give me a look of disapproval, so I continue.

"Well, I mean, I'm sure some of it must be false." She shuts down her words. "I guess, asking you about these things violates our first-date clause of no questions."

I stop close enough to her for a feeling of intimacy but not close enough to be intrusive. Just close enough that if my hand falls an inch or two too far, it may gently caress her leg. However, before I can even get to test that strategy, she pulls my move. I feel her hand casually pass over my leg, sending shivers up my spine. The subtleness of it, as she pretends nothing just happened, has my heart pumping just a little faster than it just was. Then again, maybe it was an accidental graze.

"It would be a violation of those rules. At least for now. I'll answer a more specific one if you answer a question afterward." I offer up an exchange.

She purses her lip toward her ear and scrunches her nose in quick thought. "Depends on the question," she rebuts.

I nod at the quickness of her counteroffer. "Okay. Here's the question." As I am about to say something, I feel her hand rest on my thigh—intentional and well played, though I am not exactly sure what it means. She's comfortable and maybe she's just friendly, or this could be going exactly where it is meant to go; where, now at least, I hope it goes. I forget my question for a moment as I think about her hand on my thigh, slow-moving it closer and inward. The thoughts swimming through my brain have taken the turtle entirely out of his shell. He's starting to lift his head and neck in search of his surroundings.

"Cat got your tongue?" she says, as her hand strokes my inner thigh in small, deliberate motions.

"The ... question .... is," I say in between breaths being stolen from me, "what is your occupation?" I try to word it as carefully as possible so she can't weasel her way out of an answer.

Her hand stops. She looks at me with eyes that are flooding with disappointment. Not my intentions at this moment. I did not mean for this ship to change course, but before defeat overflows from her eyes, a devilish grin takes over. She moves closer to me, turning to face me. I can feel her skin connect with mine under the water and can't help but look at her lips at this moment. A little bite of her bottom lip tells me this is going to go exactly where I now think and hope it will go. There is also a part of me wondering why it is going where it's going. Is it because she wants me or because she read about Finn Fairlane extraordinaire in some e-zine? As much as I should care about her motives, I like her, and no matter the reason she wants me, she wants me. I choose this life and can't really be too snub-nosed about why she wants me. On top of it all, it's not like Faith is knocking at my door. No, she went back to Ronnie. She went back to years of not feeling like it is actually what she wants. Whatever. Right now I have things to concentrate on.

Her hand slides over and grips my rock-hard manhood. She gently moves her hand up and down, just enough to tease me a couple of times.

A smile crosses her face. "It's nice to see you are a grower and not a show-er."

A slight chuckle escapes me. "Told you it's cold."

I wrap my hands around her and run my fingernails up and down her back. She leans in for a kiss as she climbs onto my lap. I feel her perfect breasts press against my chest. Her soft flesh against mine as the hot water flows around us causes my arousal to heighten. My man is now standing at high alert, code red, the alarm that says you must be ready at less than a moment's notice because the shit's about to get seriously real.

This kiss she gives me, it is not disarming, not like the first time. That kiss was to get out of my head any misinterpretation I might have had that first date. It worked, and it put her in control. She is still in control as her kiss explores more than just my lips. There is a deepness in her touch that pierces my soul yet is gentle enough to say that this night might be more than just the things we do for unlawful, carnal knowledge.

I pull back from this kiss and lock eyes with her. She waits in anticipation of finding out why I pulled away, not a look of disappointment but more of a yearning to know why I stopped.

"We are on uneven playing ground," I say, slowing the mood down a bit. It might not be the suavest thing I can say to control the pace of the mood, but it's all I have.

The wind picks up for a moment as she shifts back from me a tad. It sends a chill across my warm body, causing quite a jarring feeling. It takes me out of the moment for just a second. I shake it off the best I can as the wind dies back down. The clear skies above grow cloudier by the second. A distant thunder roars; no lightning though, just the clap of thunder.

"I promise I'll tell you. Don't ruin the moment," Jacquelyn says with a slight grimace.

I nod in silent understanding.

Her grimace fades away. "I just find that once people know what I do, it's the only reason they want to be with me. You understand?"

"I do, and when you tell me, then you can ask any question you want about my past," I tell her. I can't help but think that if she genuinely understands being in that situation, she wouldn't have Googled my name. Or at least she would have respected the violation enough not to have brought it up in conversation in some attempt to lure me in. But I want to enjoy the moment. I want to enjoy this encounter and this being with her. The violation of our initial agreement aside, I enjoy my time with her, and much like Viv, she doesn't seem to mind my past, or at least what she read about it.

I look into her eyes and push aside my other thoughts. I pull her close to me and connect our lips. She lets out a little exhale as she climbs back on top of my lap. I feel her skin press against mine as I become more and more aroused. She reaches down below the water and grabs my rock-hard, little man. Forget the foreplay; as Rilo Kiley sang about talking and touching, well, it leads to sex, leaving no mystery. Well, there will still be some mystery left, at least for me. Jenny Lewis may have left out kissin' in those lyrics, but their fans get the point—and right now, so do I. Jacquelyn wants it, and she wants it now.

She maneuvers herself right on top of me. I feel the warmth of her lips between her thighs as they wrap around my man. Jacquelyn is met with resistance as she tries to slide me inside. She scrunches her face as she wiggles my stick, trying to fit me inside her. There is no happy ending, at least for the moment. She flops down out of momentary frustration. I can feel myself sitting between her, my sausage snuggly wrapped in her warm, tender bun.

"I seem to be having trouble." She lets out a timid laugh, squirming around as she rubs her squeezebox on my ... well, inappropriate musical metaphor for my penis. I'd come up with one, but blood isn't flowing to my brain at the moment.

I smile at her troubles. Sex is not why I came over here tonight. It has just turned into a huge bonus … if we can make this happen.

"No worries. If at first you don't succeed … but you know this isn't why I came here tonight," I say, clearing up any misconception she may have.

Her voice quiets down. The look in her eye is shadowed by the underwater light changing to a dark blue. It gives her a menacing look, like she is about to tell a scary campfire story. She is still so beautiful in all her apparent maleficence. Her right hand is below the surface. She moves my sausage aside to play in her own playpen. I'm not sure what she is doing but who am I to stop her? "I know. It's what I wanted. I don't get to do this as often as you might think. But I want this. People look at me and see a piece of ass and a big set of tits."

"I don't think that's all true. You are very gorgeous but… " I try to say something that will boost her waning self-image, but my mind erases all the words I've ever known, making me unable to finish the thought.

She smooshes her lips against mine as my thought escapes me. The tightened eyes and raised cheeks tell me she has had this conversation before. Her left hand grabs my hand and places it over her right. I feel three fingers emerge from inside herself. She places two of mine back inside. She uses her hands to silently direct mine. I am her sex toy for the moment.

I. Am. Happy.

"It can be. But you didn't. You were respectful at the store and the concert. It impressed me," she says, pulling my hand out and going for a second attempt at insertion. "Now shut up and get inside me before the mood is ruined for good."

If there is ever a time to know when to shut up, now is it. I don't know what the hell the finger play was for, but it did something. The approach is still tight but manageable. The runway is cleared.

I. Am. In.

A thought enters my mind—no glove, and yet I am still getting love. The first thoughts that always go through a guy's mind race through mine. Is she on birth control, or are we using the ever so unreliable pull-out method? Does she have any STDs? Hell, do I have any STDs? I know I don't, but it's still something to think about. How can she trust that I just won't bust a nut inside her and have little Jacquelyns or Finns running around in nine months? I can't really answer those, but I sure as shit don't want to ask them either. One of those questions put an unwilling look on my face. She stops. She leaves me inside of her but comes to a standstill. She rests a hand on each side of my face, holding her stare with mine.

"I am on the pill, and we've been over the herpasyph," she finishes with a deep, full-tongue, passionate kiss. While those words aren't exactly a mood-setter, they do set my mind at ease. She is sharing something with me tonight; I am here for her pleasure.

The look on my face relaxes. I can feel my tension wash away as Jacquelyn gives me her reassurance on my unspoken thoughts.

She slowly moves her hips as I fill her up. The light of the moon and the underwater colors set the mood for a much more passionate encounter than I would have imagined. The occasional slight breeze further cools down the chill of the night.

Our hands caress each other's bodies, exploring wet skin as we try to find where and what pushes the right buttons. I discover some of hers in the small of her back and the inner thigh. Not too close to the fun zone, more midway down her thigh; the area that is too intimate for public, and generally the start of where you try touching to test boundaries—like the previews at the beginning of soft-core porn. This is what turns her on. No complaints from me. My fingers run behind her neck, gently touching where her hairline starts. I can feel her shiver for a moment and stop breathing. Just for a second, then she catches her breath.

"Finn," she whispers ever-so-softly in my ear. The feel of her breath on my skin sends shivers through me.

The bubbling jets of the hot tub drone out their watery approval as we stay intertwined and connected beneath the surface. But even above the roar of the jets, I can hear Jacquelyn's heart beating fast and, if beating hearts could beat in emotional tones, nervously excited. I'm sure she's done this before. She knew exactly what she was doing to get me to this point, but still, the sound echoing from her chest has newfound excitement in each rapid beat.

Her grinding against me starts to quicken. She digs her nails into my back as if she needs to hold on or else be sucked away in the vortex of a black hole. The piercing pain adds to my arousal. She bites her lower lip as I feel her tighten around my member. Her nails release as she keeps increasing her speed and pulls close to her, smashing our bodies together in an attempt to defy the laws of physics. And I say kudos to her efforts. But I am a man, and the sensations are too much. She holds me tighter as I try to pull away. I am trapped in her wild, sexual embrace.

"I can't hold…" I start to tell her, but she stops me with a deep kiss. I feel her muscles pulsate around my rock-hard sidekick.

She continues her climax as she pulls on my hair yet keeps me in for more kissing. My arms fly down to my side as I can't hold out any longer. My pelvis thrusts upward as I cum hard inside her.

She rests down on me for a moment as she writhes around, playing with my man still in her. She smiles while looking around at the patio furniture behind me and the yard and space beyond the lanai.

"You're not as … vocal as I thought you'd be," she says, still scanning the surrounding area.

"Same can be said of you," I reply.

"Private moments are meant to be private. You don't always want to be the main attraction, do ya?" she says, returning to me. She slides off of me and stands out of the hot water.

As she wraps herself in a towel and heads on in to clean herself up, I can't help but think about what she said. *Do I always want to be the main attraction? Could that be my issue? Faith, Viv, now Jacquelyn.* In some way, could there be something inside of me that craves to have every girl helplessly fall for me, like some nineties song about love letters in the sand?

I do know that tonight wasn't about rekindling some long-lost love, nor was the excitement with her about the possibility of being caught by restaurant patrons or throwing a bone to a long-time fan. It wasn't even about her fulfilling some long-time teenage fantasy. It was about the moment; it was about us.

I sit alone in the hot tub as I watch the few clouds above pass by, covering stars as they do. The infinite abyss above me, and bubbling water around me, and all I can think about is the girl a couple dozen feet away from me cleaning herself up. I don't know much about her. She only knows slightly more about me. But I do know that until this thought, Faith had been out of my mind.

Maybe that's my problem. I always have and always will come back to Faith. Every thought, every action, everything I do, eventually, for better or worse, will be done with her in mind.

From inside, I hear the unmistakable organ notes resonate and the lyrics that immediately follow suit as she hits play on her stereo. A girl who, in this day and age, still uses a real record player and stereo set-up, not some iPod dock connected to what now passes as quality desktop speakers. As Madonna sings outs from inside, I know that this girl, Jacquelyn, is a mystery, one that apparently stands alone. The problem is that when I hear her call my name, it doesn't feel like home. But the sadness that flows through me right now is that I want it to feel like home. There is this woman who has given herself to me, if only for a night, and seems so sincere and real in what she does, even if she does seem a bit apprehensive about letting me into her world.

So now, in a matter of months, I find myself caught twice between my undying feelings for Faith and another woman. This one doesn't seem to mind my past and wants to be with me for other reasons than who I once was or how much money she thinks I have. But unlike Jacquelyn, Faith doesn't seem to want to be with me. Maybe this time I won't have the opportunity to mess this up with my lovingly disastrous ways.

I open my eyes to the harsh light of day. As the world comes into focus and my mind clears away the fog of sleep, I remember I am not in my own bed. She is gone: up, awake, and somewhere that is not within eyesight. Clear in my mind are the events of last night that led into today: the hot tub, the wine, the sex, and the bedroom afterward.

Everything that is running through my mind right now are thoughts I've had at one point or another about one woman or another. But now, I am comfortable thinking these thoughts: feelings of uncertainty and being okay with that—true desire for someone other than Faith. It is strange not to fight these thoughts and hold onto the possibilities of what my mind thinks could be with Faith, to let go of those, at least for the moment so I can ponder the possibilities with Jacquelyn. You know, before I unconsciously and inevitably mess things up here to leave open the possibility there.

I cross my arms behind my head and stare at the MC Escher mounted on the wall across from her bed. I think if art says anything about the character of a person, this piece is pretty much my life. The stairs that are leading everywhere, with no real direction to any one place yet, while boggling the mind to comprehend the spatial reasoning does make sense in the chaos. If I can relate to that, then maybe she does too, and that's why I feel the connection to her.

The chaos of it all hits me. One week until the wedding and only an extra five days until the tour starts. So much to do still and here I lay, in a new girl's bed, trying to figure out the meaning of life. It brings a smile to my face because no matter how many times I've been in this exact situation of lying in some girl's bed the next day, contemplating the meaning of it all, it is never the same. The meanings I find in the previous night's events are never the same. No two women are ever the same, and thus why my next day's contemplation is never the same. So, I lay, trying to figure it out but there is a nudge in my mind, a nudge that makes my subconscious speak aloud to me, that this time I shouldn't overthink it. The voice inside my head whispers to me that I should just let it be. Perhaps this is what she was trying to get across to me at the concert.

But here's the thing, I can't just let it be. Everything I've done since I met her has been for her. Her being the capital H. The F A I T H. Everything since we've broken up has been because I've had thoughts about her, thoughts about what could still be, or what could have been, to put it more realistically. Ideas put into lyrics about regrets of things said and done, songs about my, and the great human, inability to move on because we know how wonderfully fantastic things could be if we could just get it right—like an artist continually tweaking the hairline of a portrait to make sure the resemblance is absolutely perfect—we strive and strive to make things right so they can be everything we ever hoped to be. But more often than not, things are not what we expected. Things do not turn out like we thought they would. They turn out how they turn out and, more often than not, the way they turn out is well below our expectations of where we think it should be. I look around at how it has turned out for me.

I look around this room at the MC Escher and to the antique dresser with a vanity mirror connected to, what I assume, is some sort of makeup lighting concoction. I look up to the ceiling at the off-white color needing to be repainted and think about how my life turned out exactly like I always wanted. I wanted the music. I wanted the fame and the fortune, the weeks in and out of hotels and long nights on the road, all of it. But when you want all these things, and you are working toward these things, you don't think about, because you can't see, what will get left behind. You can't foresee what will get damaged in the process; the things that get hurt that, one way or another, leave you scarred and a little less human.

The smell of bacon and coffee waft into the room from under the door. I take a deep breath and enjoy the aroma. I reach over the side of the bed and grab my shirt and pants. I figure with the tour mostly planned and ready to go, I can take care of smaller details after eating a filling, late breakfast.

As I pull my shirt over my head, I hear the sound of footsteps and the door to the bedroom open. My top pulls down over my eyes to see Jacquelyn standing there, looking radiant and far too awake no matter what hour it is.

"Thought maybe you worked up an appetite." She extends the tray my direction.

I straighten myself as I pull up my jeans. She walks the tray to me.

"Thank you. Smells delicious," I note.

She places the tray on my lap and takes a seat at my feet. I dig into my food and coffee.

"I don't care about your past. It's what you do now that I care about. It's what you do today that makes you a good man or a bad one." She doesn't mean to, I'm sure, but she sounds like the beginning of a motivational speech in some coming-of-age film.

I stop eating and raise a brow to her words, waiting for her to say more. "I had fun," she continues. "I have fun every night we are together, and I'm not sure how I feel about that."

Not the most promising way to end what I'm guessing is her attempt at some sort of confession. I wait some more to see what else is on her mind.

"I mean, I'm not normally the dating type. Life's led me down a more 'love-em-and-leave-em' path." She hesitates, as if I may cringe at those words. "But with you, it's different. It feels different. More comfortable and yet uncomfortable at the same time. I'm not sure how to put it into words, really."

I swallow the last bite from my pile of bacon and set the tray aside. Before I say anything, it dawns on me that she generally doesn't cook, either for herself or others, as my entire breakfast tray consisted of about half a pound of almost overcooked bacon and coffee. No eggs, no pancakes or waffles, just bacon, which leads me to believe she was happy I stuck around. This is her attempt to do something nice, which also leads me to believe that whatever she does for a living, it is not cooking.

But back in the moment with her, I find some words. "New. The word you are looking for to describe your feeling is new."

She shakes her head in short bursts of agreement without breaking eye contact. I grab her hand. "Whatever you find you need out of this thing we have going on, it's okay. You don't have to figure it all out right now. I'm not going to ghost you or cut you out."

I feel my phone buzz in my pocket, and I know she hears the quiet commotion too because the look in her eyes shifts out from wherever she was lost in and back to her bedroom. Her eyes almost look sad for a moment as she is brought back to the reality that we can't lay in bed forever.

I pull out my phone, figuring it's some email confirmation on one of the hotel/motel stays we have on the tour. But no, this moment with Jacquelyn couldn't end uneventfully. It has to be interrupted by a text from Faith—cryptic and vague.

[Faith: Meet me at the patio. I'll have a drink waiting for you.]

[Finn: I have a few errands. Tour shit. Be there this evening.]

[Faith: I'll be there.]

Life can't ever be easy. I have come to learn that's the way the universe works, at least for me. I can't enjoy this moment of newfound feelings Jacquelyn has for me. I can't be relishing in it with her because now I have Faith on my mind, poking away at me. Jacquelyn knows it too. She sees it on my face—a tenseness that wasn't there before I read the text.

Jacquelyn stands, distancing herself from me. "Let me guess: you have to go?" She hammers that nail dead center on the head. Her face falls as all happiness she just felt is washed away by the cynical beast resurfacing. Her immediate composure starts to shut me out as she stands there, trying with failing effort not to cross her arms.

"Yes. But there's nothing to worry about. I have to go meet someone, probably about the tour or her sister's impending doom with irrational, preconceived notions of love and marriage," I say, trying to calm her growing nerves. "Want to meet up tonight sometime?"

Her arms uncross, and a new sort of uncomfortableness clouds over her. "I can't tonight. I have to … work."

"Ah, the elusive work topic. I see. Well, if you want, call me afterward. We can have a late dinner or early breakfast, if you'd like," I offer up.

A smile crosses her face for the first time since she heard the rattle of my buzzing phone. "I'm sorry. I get that way sometimes. Comes with the territory."

"You don't have to apologize for who you are. You don't owe me an explanation. I'm just happy you like me enough to get jealous over suspicion," I say, calming her nerves. "May I use your shower before I go?"

She nods as she walks me to her bathroom. "Of course. You don't mind if I join, do you?"

The hot water ran over our bodies, causing scenes from last night's hot tub adventures to replay in my head. My eyes were focused on her, bringing my mind back to the present. Her toned abs, an outline of a six-pack starting to shine through. She definitely gets her exercise.

She presses her perfect breasts against me as she moves in for a deep, passionate kiss. I love the feeling of her skin pressed against mine. The water makes small pools where it can, cascading down our bodies in little waterfalls.

Now, in any standard shower sex scenario, I'd turn her around, smack her ass, and fuck her from behind, watching the shower water bounce off her perfectly sculpted ass, but there is passion in the air, a new flavor of romance dancing on my tongue this moment that says, "not facing away. Not doggie style." I want to keep it more personal. There's a long-lost emotion that has awakened in my mind that wants something more.

Right behind her are built-in shelves for soap and shampoo. Perfect footrests for me to try new shower adventures. I turn around so the water runs over her. I don't need the warmth right now, and cleanliness can wait till this is over. I run my hands down her back as she strokes my ego, making it bigger and ready for action. I place one hand on each of her ass cheeks and firmly grip down, hoisting her up. Her feet catch on the makeshift footrests now behind me. She is either a quick learner or has done this before. She holds onto me with her left arm while aligning our fun parts with her right.

I slide inside her, smooth and easy. I hear her take a short, deep breath and tense around me, the familiar feel of someone being pleasured by me. The sensation only adds to my growing feelings for her.

As she slowly wiggles and slides around on my (what Lady Gaga so eloquently refers to as) Disco Stick, I realize that my feelings for Jacquelyn might be growing faster and have a farther reach than I feel I am ready for. Only once before have I fallen for someone in such a short amount of time, which brings me back to where I am supposed to be heading—Faith.

"Shit," I say out loud, thinking I am going to have one pissed-off ex on my hands if I take too long.

"It's okay. Like I said, I'm on the pill," Jacquelyn responds to what she thinks is me about to send my little guys marching on.

But I take the misinterpretation to try and speed things along. I concentrate on her moist warmth that surrounds my member. I look down as she thrusts her pelvis back and forth, forcing me to fill her up. I look at her to see her staring at me, which excites me in new ways. She speeds up her grinding as I feel, even in the showering waters, the spilling of her juices all over me. I feel them run down my leg, intertwining with the shower water. She bites her bottom lip as she tries not to deafen me with her screams. I can't hold it anymore; her permission to land has been received. My body tenses for a moment before it all involuntarily relaxes, including my grip on her bottom. She slides off my rock-hard erection as I accidentally drop her; an accident that shoots massive amounts of unwanted pain in my special place.

She makes quick work of her feet and pads her fall as I try to regain my grip on her. It works just enough that her somewhat gentle landing leaves her unharmed on the shower floor. I, on the other hand, manage to hold myself up just long enough to make sure she is safe before sliding down in searing pain.

She has this look on her face as she giggles like a forest nymph. She is not laughing at my pain but at the comedy in the situation. It makes me start to chuckle, which does not help relieve any of the pain, but she is just too beautiful as the shower rains down on her to not laugh along.

"So much for going out with a bang today," she says through her laugh.

I crinkle my nose, nodding at her statement, as I collect myself as much as I can. She stays down there, looking at me, even though I turn off the shower. As she smiles, I see in her eyes someone who looks content. I always said contentment is next to godliness. So, I'll take the happy look in her eye as I dry myself off with the towel that was flung over the shower door.

And yes, I know what you are thinking. Cleanliness is next to godliness, but if there is a god and you stand next to him, I think contentment would be the first feeling that comes to mind, not, "Boy, do I feel clean." That's what showers are for.

"Can you turn the shower back on for me, Finn?" Jacquelyn asks as I step out. I oblige, leaving her happy and content in the indoor rainstorm.

"Call me later tonight?" I ask, heading out of the bathroom.

"I'm out late. Is that okay?" Jacquelyn shouts from under the stream of water.

"Of course." I make my way down the hall.

I don't want to leave right now. What I want is not to have a throbbing penis that is hurting because it was just bent close to a 45-degree angle while rock-hard. What I want is to be with her in the shower, holding her or, at least, pulling her hair. But as I said, I have to go to the woman to whom I will always be a slave.

CHAPTER 10

Broken Things

The night air is calm as I enter the patio section of our old haunt. I see Faith sitting there by herself, away from any crowd. Her only company is the drink she has waiting for me. None of the usual suspects are around. Sure, there are other people, non-players in my world taking up space around me: the regulars we know only from here but never see anywhere else and the usual staff. They laugh, talk, drink, and go about their world without concern for what is happening in mine. I don't mean anything contemptible by that. I go around every day without more than a general concern for what happens in other people's lives. I think we all wish people well in a unified notion that humans are, by nature, not assholes. We just don't go out of our way to make sure every stranger we encounter is happy and taken care of. If we did, homelessness would be much less a thing. But I digress.

Faith sits there and connects eyes with me as I approach. There is something I can already see simmering just below her surface, waiting to come to a boil.

She hands me my drink as I get within arm's reach. I start with a sip of the now watered-down libation, before taking it all down to save the integrity of what was once a good drink.

"Took you long enough," Faith starts. "Everything all right?"

"Perfect. I'll tell ya, if anyone asked me ten years ago, hell, even three months ago if I could ever be truly happy with someone who wasn't Faith Siubhal, I would have laughed in their face. This new girl. There's somethin' there. I can't explain it, but it's there. I would never have thought you pushing me away would actually work out for both of us. You back with Ronnie, giving it the good ol' college try. Me, happy and content for whatever it is we have. I didn't know I could feel that with someone other than you."

As I finish my last sentence, I realize that everything I just said either sounded way too manic, like I'm losing my mind or, more likely, like some backhanded way to brag to her about how I feel right now. From the look on her face, she is not as joyful about my new-found happiness as I am. She forces out a smile to hide the truth I just saw. I'm not purposefully sounding mean or trying to dig at her. She asked; I told. Then again, she is the one who pushed me away and said she was getting back with Ronnie, so I shouldn't feel guilty over my happiness; maybe I feel bad that my happiness seems to make her less happy right now.

Whatever the reason for the way she feels, I need to give her a chance to speak. So, I bring it around. "How are things with Ronnie?"

She smiles a quick smile and stands up. "Let's take a walk."

"Where did you want to go?" I inquire.

"Anywhere but here," she says, starting off the patio and toward Highway 192.

Where we are on 192 is part of the main thoroughfare. A seafood restaurant is across the street, next to a hotel and discount gift shop. Next to where we are is a jungle-themed miniature golf course. I've not played it myself, but that's not saying I won't. And, of course, next to the mini-golf course is yet another staple of the greater Orlando area—another discount gift shop. The sidewalks that line 192 are sprinkled with tourists and locals making pilgrimages to various destinations around the area. It does remind me of Reno. The streetlights and neon signs of the surrounding buildings guide our way as we stroll down 192.

We stop at a parking lot exit as a crowded SUV pulls out to make a right. Faith looks at me, "So, you really like this new girl?"

I let out a smile, one that comes so naturally just thinking about the mystery that is Jacquelyn. "Yeah. I do. She's ... uncomplicated. Or at least that's how things are right now. It's nice. Comfortable."

Faith lets out a quiet chuckle before walking on.

"Maybe not uncomplicated," I backtrack, causing a raised eyebrow from Faith. "Well, yeah, uncomplicated but mysterious."

She continues staring at me with a hint of a smile trying to cross her lips.

I know she needs a little more so I say the only thing I can think of. "It's complicated."

She shakes her head at my unraveling of the whole thing.

"Not the relationship. Understanding it is complicated." A feeble and failed attempt to clarify.

She only shakes her head, looking upward into the night sky.

"It's funny," she says.

"What is?" I respond.

"The universe, life, everything," she says, the weight of her words causing her to sigh.

I am enjoying this little moment with her, even though I'm not sure where she is going with this. I too look up toward the sky and the infinite beyond, trying to see what she is looking at.

She continues her ponderance. "The vastness of it all. To think that within the scope of existence, we are not in the same spot of the universe we were when we first met. Not just that Earth travels around the sun but that the sun moves throughout the universe, on a straight path forward." She pauses for a moment, just staring into the night. "But we don't realize we travel. To us, we feel like we've not moved. But try to imagine how far we've come." She looks forward again and continues walking. "Did you ever think we'd end up here?"

The gravity of her words hits hard. I'm searching for the right thing to say, but I'm not sure there is anything to say. I think her words are things to ingest and let take over your body. It's thoughts like those that made her my muse. The ideas, dreams, and notions of life she has can still instill inspiration without even trying. She is magical. So, I enjoy this walk with her.

"Hell, I always thought it would turn out differently," I admit in a moment of raw truth. "Did you think it would have led to this?"

She smiles and gives me a soft huff. "Had you asked me that back in college, I would have thought I'd be living in a subdivision somewhere. I'd be working somewhere, marketing probably. But that changed. Had someone asked me after I finished cosmetology school what I would be doing, I would have thought I'd be some hotshot salon owner by now, rakin' in the dough. But as it turns out, I make a good living doing what I do and don't have to deal with owning a salon."

"Never thought about the end of you and me?" I put out there.

"Sure. Once, it was all I thought about, especially right after we broke up. I wanted to turn around and see your smile that told me everything would be just fine." Faith turns to see me smile. She points to me. "That smile. Right there. I dreamt a thousand times of that smile saving me. But it never came around. I never heard from you. I only kept up on you through magazine interviews and radio shows. So, I moved on. But I always figured in the end, if it was meant to be, it would be."

The words she speaks do not bring much relief to my soul. I don't feel saved or redeemed. I feel like those words told me that everything I did between our break-up and now has been misguided. Maybe that's life—just a series of foolish steps trying to do the right thing. Hell, I don't even know how to respond to something like that.

"I wish I knew. I would have run back," I say.

"But it's that you didn't know that made me able to move on," she says. Those last words slay the demon that has been taunting me, and possibly her, for two decades.

We continue to walk in comfortable silence for a few moments as we make our way farther down the street. We feel ourselves being sucked into the tourist-trapping lights of 192. I am not sure if it is the proverbial flame of the neon lights pulling us in like moths or something more, but she has yet to speak on whatever the subject is she wanted to talk about. I'm not going to force her to speak either. When she wants to chat about it, she will. It's just pleasant being with her: no big news or life-changing event is happening; no sexual tension waiting to snap; no anger aimed at either of us; no animosity brewing beneath the surface. All cards laid out. All our chips cashed in. Just two friends who are enjoying a moment together.

"Ronnie's coming to the party, right?" I finally break the silence after a few, long moments.

"What party?" Faith says, watching traffic whiz by.

"The bachelor party. I figure the past is the past, and if you and him are good, then I should be good with him." I know it sounds cheap and tawdry. I don't care; it's not. Our lives are intertwined and have been, even the years we were apart. If this guy's going to be in her life, then he's going to be in mine. I might as well make the best of it.

She thinks for a moment, making a few contorted faces as she gathers her thoughts. While I didn't think my original question or clarifying statement that followed was confusing or misleading, something in my words set off something in her mind that is causing a sort of internal confusion.

After a few, short moments of her face finding its way back to normal, she manages to say, "Yeah. I think so. I'll ask him. I thought you already invited him."

"I don't know. I may have. I'm just making conversation. Not really sure what else is going on in your head and thought words needed to be spoken." That's crap, kind of. I wanted to be nice and make sure he's coming. A friend of my friend is not my enemy, so why not embrace it? She might be right though. I may have invited him already.

"So, the tour is all laid out?" she pipes in.

"Yeah, looks like Logan Square will be doing at least all the East Coast stops with Spear Fist. Maybe more, but that can be played by ear for a bit," I offer up, trying to add some sort of enthusiasm to the quiet that surrounds us.

"I'd suggest clearing the air of any lingering whatevers that might still be hanging around between you and Viv," Faith says in an all-too-wordy response.

"I don't think there's anything to clear," I say, looking across the street at a couple of random teenagers meandering about a parking lot.

"No lingering emotions? Nothing to say to her about the turnabout in the bushes with Logan?" Faith pries.

I shake my head. "Honestly, nothing going on there."

"If you're sure," she prods.

"I'm not sure what you want me to say. Admit some lingering feelings of hopeless romanticism toward her and how I wish we were still together? She broke it off and for good reasons." I try to shut her down, but still she pokes.

"What reasons were those?"

I stop walking on the sidewalk near some parking lot entrance. The lights of the stores behind Faith turn her into a silhouette. "She said that if she stayed with me, she'd be with me, but I would be with her and you, at least emotionally. Is that what you want to hear?"

"It's not about what I want to hear, Finn. It's about the truth." She turns back to continue walking. "So, is it true?"

I stay silent for a moment, thinking about my words. Rare moments allow me to choose them wisely. I think because in these rare moments, my mind knows I am most likely going to have to eat them. "True? Yeah. Always. But you know that, so I don't know why you need to hear it from me."

She laughs a hard but honest laugh. It's a laugh that starts in the stomach and works its way out to help save the brain from the pain and aggravation of what you are about to say. "Do I? When we were together back in the day, how many other girls were there?"

She pauses and looks at me. The look in her eyes demands that I do not answer. I just take a deep breath, indicating that she should go on.

"Even now, after we … reconnected or whatever, how many girls? How is it that you love me? How is it that you have all these feelings for me? Feelings that place me so high on some holy pedestal, making me untouchable and infallible in your eyes? I need to know. These aren't rhetorical."

A car obnoxiously blares its horn as it whizzes by, the music that raged out of the open window partly drowned out by the loud blast of the horn. The dark, with all the surrounding artificial light, silhouettes the car and hides the mysterious driver. But it takes me out of the moment, if only for a second.

"Well?" Faith says, further prodding me for an answer.

"Of course. But I don't hold you on some infallible pedestal. Make no mistake of that. I know that you, just like me, are fully capable of fucking things up without trying. I love you not even in spite of that great ability but love you more because of it. I never needed a perfect woman. I've made my mistakes, but you were always the right thing. You were always the one choice I made that I knew was right. You, Faith. No one else. But you asked me to stop. With no uncertain words, you said, 'it's over.'"

"Is it ever really over between us?" she says.

Those words make the universe stop. Every planet and star have stopped in their paths. The question that, if answered, would give me the answer to life itself. Is it ever really over? Only time will tell. But knowing that it won't be answered here and now, the universe moves forward.

I look at her. In the reflection of the neon lights, I can see tears running down her face.

"I don't see why you needed to know all this anyway," I say. "You got your guy back. But here's the thing. In the short few months I've been down here, I've made a family. D.B., Vince, Neil, Gregg, Viv, you, hell, even Jeanine. You guys are all my family. So, I might always love you, and that's fine. That's for me to deal with. I won't pursue you. I won't bug you. I won't bother you or remind you of what could have been. I got your message. But you are part of that group, and we are all on the same path in the same caravan. I can deal with that."

She starts walking through the parking lot toward a Baskin Robbins/Dunkin Donuts shop. At this hour, I'm not sure if she's looking for a sugar fix or hit of caffeine. I'm just along for the ride.

She turns to me and stops just outside the door. "It all matters, Finn. It matters more than you know."

We both reach for the handle at the same time, causing our hands to touch. Nothing we haven't done a thousand times before, but there is a spark. She pulls away too fast, like a reaction to static shock.

"Wasn't there something you wanted to tell me? Isn't that why we went on this walk in the first place?" I ask, letting go of the door.

The same honk from moments ago sounds again from a car entering the lot. This time, the lights of the buildings illuminate the racing stripe on the blue Camaro that is undeniably Ronnie's.

"Hey, you guys!" he shouts from the window, unintentionally sounding like Sloth from *The Goonies*. I might not have anything against the guy; it's just that he sure makes the shots easy to take sometimes.

He pulls into a parking space with the force of a stunt driver testing the limits of the car's brakes. He hops out and lumbers our way.

Faith turns to me and smiles a tiny, half-smile. "Yeah, I do. Another time though."

"Thought I was s'posed to meet you for beers?" Ronnie says in a way that conveys his less-than-intellectual mind.

She smiles for him. "Yeah, just decided I wanted some ice cream. Thought I'd make it back before you got there."

He nods at her—an indication her answer was acceptable to him, though I'm not sure what would have happened if it wasn't. He turns to me. A quick thought enters my mind that I should either run, run so far away or start round two of a losing battle, but a more mature idea dominates my actions. I extend my hand out in greetings.

"Nice to see you, Ronnie," I start.

He looks down and half-heartedly shakes my hand, "Finn. Keeping your paws to yourself."

I casually let go of his grip. I don't want to come across as defensive. I also don't want to maintain a handshake with a man who still holds a grudge. It might be a legit grudge but still a grudge, nonetheless.

"No hard feelings, I hope." An earnest response, hoping to diffuse any further momentum.

"Nah, man. I won." Ronnie sneers his lip while flexing his pecs beneath his white tank top.

There's a part of me that wonders what Faith doesn't see in herself or what she does see that makes her feel so inferior or so undeserving of someone better than him. I'm not saying that someone better is me. I can hope it's me, but I'm just saying anyone better than the oversized neanderthal that is Ronnie Frown. And while I can understand how he got that nickname, I can't help but wonder if that's the surname he signs now.

"I trust you're coming to the bachelor party?" I ask, trying to bring the conversation around to something slightly more comfortable for Faith, and to help this brute move beyond the image of my little guy in her behind.

"Hell yeah. It'll be…" Ronnie pauses for a moment, and at that moment, all I can think to myself is, *Don't say it. Please don't say it.* A small hope that he has some original thought in his mind, but he says it anyway, "Legendary." For the love of all that is holy, a phrase that has been well established and now wholly unoriginal in usage just spewed forth from this man's mouth. The only person among the more than seven billion people on God's green earth that can say that phrase and not be called unoriginal is NPH. On the other hand, Ronnie's right. Legendary it shall be.

"Good. Then let's get some ice cream and head back to the bar," I say, holding the door open for them.

"Ladies first." I wave my hand for Faith to enter first. Ronnie follows behind her with a quick slap on her behind.

She jumps from the unexpected slap and shakes her head, presumably at the juvenileness of his action. Though, the look on her face reads, to me at least, that this is the man she has consigned herself to. We grab a quick couple scoops of ice cream. She orders orange sherbet and I peanut butter and chocolate. Ronnie buys some monstrous sundae topped with everything they have behind the counter. The good news for me is that if he eats like this on a regular basis, I won't have that many years to wait until he drops dead of a heart attack.

For now, however, we climb into his monstrosity of a muscle car and cruise back to the patio bar we love so much. The quick two-minute ride is filled not with any sort of intellectual or enlightening conversation, but instead, our ears are graced with the gravely sounds of some Lamb of God-style vocalist. Not bad music by any means, but not the mood-setter to end what lack of conversation Faith and I didn't have.

Our short trip out for ice cream is enough time to fill the patio with the usual suspects: D.B., Gregg, Jeanine, Vincent, Neil, Viv, and Logan, all relaxing around the red-cushioned, plastic wicker furniture that makes this spot so homey. As if walking into a scene from month's past, D.B., dressed to the nines with his leather-studded wristband, is swaying a beer around in exaggerated motions as he tells some story to a crowd of mesmerized onlookers. Again, I think to myself that these people could probably not care less about him if he weren't who he is and who he is going to become shortly. Then again, he is who he is. So, enjoy the moment, good sir, for they are fleeting and few as the years go by.

D.B. sees us enter the patio and his storytelling stops as his eyes turn to the three of us. He wets his throat with the rest of his beer as he stands up, waving us over.

I hear D.B. say to the crowd of spectators, "This is who I was talking about. The man, the myth: the one, the only Finn Fairlane."

Some girl from the crowd who reminds me a bit of Faith from our heyday pipes up, "Wait a minute, bruh. All of that over a girl? No way would a girl ever go through that for some dick."

D.B. turns to the young woman, who after saying "bruh" makes me think her driver's license was purchased from a frat boy for fifty bucks, and retorts, "Ask him yourself." He then turns to me, slinging his free arm around my shoulder. His beer breath makes me slightly intoxicated. "Finn, I was just regaling some tales of yore. These fine folks don't believe me when I tell them of your exploits!"

I excuse the fact that he sounds like a pirate onto his second or third bottle of rum and turn my attention to the crowd for a moment.

I give the crowd a humble smile. "I'm sure whatever D.B. said is either oddly true or wildly exaggerated. Your choice as to what to believe." I turn to the man that has helped me stay relevant and whisper in his ear, "You get the stripper lined up?"

"Just one?" D.B. laughs. "No, my friend. I got three!" He pats me on the back while laughing. "The stories from the party will need to be epic enough that they live on in the hearts of all men!"

"Gregg! Come here," I shout while waving my hand.

He gets up from sitting next to his fiancé and, after planting a huge kiss on her lips, walks to us.

"Nice to see you, Finn," Gregg starts. "Very excited to see what you all have in store."

"Me too. It seems that D.B. has made some adjustments to the plans," I say.

"As long as I have plausible deniability, Jeanine can't be mad," Gregg clarifies.

"All good, mate. You know nothing!" D.B. sounds even more like a pirate than moments ago.

I turn to Gregg. "Has he been watching a lot of pirate movies?"

"Had a marathon earlier today. He's on a kick," Gregg replies.

"Well, then. Yo ho ho and a bottle of rum!" I shout, flinging my arm around D.B.'s shoulder. "Next round on me!"

As we all sit regaling stories of yesteryear, I can't help but notice that Faith, as happy as she says she is with Ronnie, giving their relationship another shot, doesn't have the look on her face of someone who is ecstatic to be with their significant other. The look on her face might be signaling something more. I would go talk to her and find out what's bothering her, but she told me no. She said she wanted to be with him. So, who am I to fix her problems? Of course, if she said anything, I would in a second. But she hasn't, and quite honestly, I can't get Jacquelyn out of my mind.

The hours pass, and the restaurant finally closes down. We all sit in quieter moods as our last drinks have been drunk. The winds from the day have all but stopped. Hell, even the traffic seems not to be as noisy. The staff has come to terms with us sitting on the patio after closing, with locked doors restricting our access to bathrooms. It is the point of the night that as people find the need for the facilities, they find themselves in their cars heading to wherever the night leads them. As the numbers dwindle down, I am surprised to find it down to just Faith, D.B., and myself. D.B., though, is passed out across one of the red-cushioned love seats.

I watch Faith as she sits almost uncomfortably, like a child who wants to speak up but doesn't know if talking is allowed. I don't want to be the first to speak on this. I do wonder where her man ran off to. This late at night, leaving her alone doesn't seem like the gentlemanly thing to do. Not that anyone here is a threat. However, in this area, you hear stories, and I wouldn't want my lady, whether it be Jacquelyn, Faith, Viv, whoever, to be on the nightly news in some tragic story.

A buzzing in my pocket interrupts my less-than-pleasant thoughts with a welcome invitation from Jacquelyn: *Come on over if you'd like*. No need to ask me twice. I nudge D.B. to wake him, but he is passed out cold. I decide it best to let sleeping D.B. lie and save the goodbye for those in the land of the woke.

"I gotta get back to Jacquelyn," I say to Faith, as I turn from D.B. "You just gonna stay here all night?"

She smiles her sad smile and shakes her head. "I was hoping to talk to you about something."

"I remember. It's why we took our walk that got interrupted. Then you said, 'another time,'" I recap. "I've been here all night. You have said nothing." I realize that may have sounded like an attack. It is not meant to come off like that. It's just that she has been avoiding me all night, and now that I get up to leave, she suddenly remembers.

"It's not when I meant to make this happen," she defends.

"Whatever it is, I'm sure it is great news for you and not going to be such great news for me. Anyway it goes, news that must be told to me directly by you doesn't have the glow of something that is going to overcome me with joy. So, can this wait for when I'm not tired and can handle stabbing news with a bit more aplomb?"

Faith nods and smiles. "Yeah, Finn. I gotta figure out where my man went off to anyway." She gets out her phone and starts texting him.

I lean in and give Faith a friendly kiss on her forehead. When my lips meet her skin, I can feel her shiver just a tad, not too much but just enough to say there is more to explore. However, now is not the time to pry or read too deep into things, so I leave it, and her, to the remaining night.

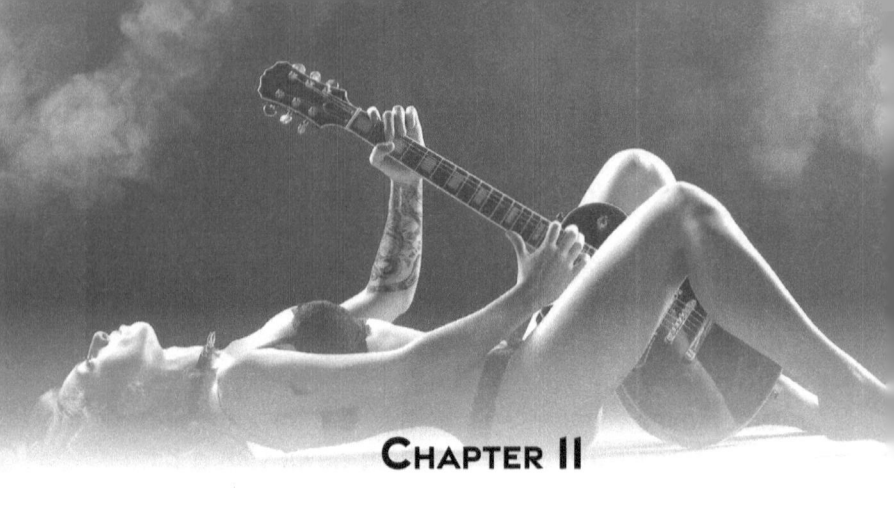

CHAPTER II

Life Is a Highway

Life's got a funny way of working out sometimes. You see someone, and you don't know why but something is nudging you deep inside that says you have to say hi. You don't know why, but you do. You follow that instinct. A friendship is formed, or possibly two lovers have just said hello. Life sometimes points things out to you like it pointed out Florida for me, signs that keep popping up over and over again, like the number twenty-three. It's nothing you can place your finger on, but it seems so right that anything else is just wrong. You can feel it anywhere you are, at any time, without notice. Here, in Florida, on this peninsula of impossible weather, it happens more often than one would imagine. This phenomenon is not just about meeting potential lovers or friends. It's about the number of small businesses that flourish here against all odds. It's about Florida Man and things that could only happen here in the land of alligators, meth, and sunshine. The invisible hand of fate that guides you along the path of life seems to favor this state and its residents.

But that's how it's been for the last few days. Every moment spent with Jacquelyn seems to be those moments guided by the hand of fate. *La Forza Del Destino*. We haven't been doing anything that would seem paramount. We haven't even left her apartment in three days. But every moment since I exited the patio without news has seemed to be guided by a force not of my own. I am okay with that.

The plans for the tour and the bachelor party are all in place. I am left with next to nothing on the agenda. My to-do list is down to having a talk with Gregg and no other deadlines. Jacquelyn had a few days off, so we decided to make the most of it. Our time was divided relatively evenly between her bedroom and the kitchen. There is something very relaxing about lounging in bed, holding the person you are falling for. And I was falling … fast. It's not been that long since I met Jacquelyn, but still, I find myself more and more fascinated by her. My thoughts are con-tinually leading back to her in the moments between making love. Ideas of what-if and could-be situations all seem happier if she's in the picture. The thought of her not being around darkens all the colors of my mind. While rock 'n roll is known for black clothes and dark makeup, those shades just don't seem like colors to describe us two. Jacquelyn is definitely a door I don't want painted black.

But here's a hue that does darken Jacquelyn and me … Faith. The nagging feeling in the back of my mind—the what-if. The should've, could've, would've that is my history both real and imagined with Faith. We are two intertwined souls on this life that is a highway, and yes, even now while I am with Jacquelyn, I want to ride it with Faith.

All. Night. Long.

It's a struggle, a war within my head, a devil on one shoulder and angel on the other. I try pushing my thoughts aside, the little voice inside my head that tells me Faith is the one, the cosmic intertwining, but I can't. Even though when we are together, I've become better at playing the role of uninterested, I still am. I've started treating her like I've treated so many one-night stands over the years, as if she's disposable. That's not what I meant to do, but I guess it's what we've boiled down to for now. And for now, I really do love, or what mixed emotions can be confused for love, Jacquelyn.

Day three of our mini-staycation, and we once again find ourselves exploring each other's bodies. This round, we decided that making cake while making love seemed like a fun way to multitask.

We both face the bowl of unmixed flour, sugar, egg, butter, and vanilla. Jacquelyn stays bent over in front of me, trying to hold the electric mixer in the ingredients, while I glide in and out of her from behind. She turns the beater on high, causing a bit of flour, egg, and sugar to splash out of the bowl. I help her steady her hand and get the beater deep inside all the mixings. We slowly mixed the batter, hand on hand, as we continued making love. The eggs blend with the flour and sugar, forming a paste that the butter warms up to and begs to be a part of. The vanilla swirls around, slowly enveloped by the rest. All the ingredients merge into one tasty, decadent treat. We continue mixing it together as we both reach our own climaxes, a perfect finish to making the batter.

As my endorphins calm down and the fantasies of the past three days dim in my head, reality sets back in. A few different thoughts rush in my mind as I stare down at her beautiful, perfect, heart-shaped ass. I have to leave this moment; I have one last duty before the tour—the bachelor party. But another thought enters my mind, one from years prior. A thought of buying my car, of being on that lot and test-driving the car before I bought my current one. I know where this thought is going, and I don't like it.

My beautiful Grand Am almost wasn't mine. I saw the green shine in the sun a few cars down from where I had currently been standing. The car in front of me, keys in hand, ready for a test-drive was a Porsche Boxster, and it was beautiful. By all standards, the Porsche was a superior car to the green Grand Am that glistened for me under the sun, so I had to test it out. The salesman seemed to want me to want this car. I wanted to want it. So, we took it out. It was beauteous. The engine purred like a kitten. The leather seats were as comfortable on my ass as any pair of breasts I had ever rested my head on. We took off out of that lot like a bat out of hell. It cornered beautifully and stopped on a dime. I had no reason not to buy that car. It was priced reasonably for a Porsche. It had no visible damage. Now I'm not a mechanic, so I didn't know what to look for under the hood that indicates wear and tear that will need replacing sooner rather than later.

So yes, I should have walked off that lot the proud new owner of a Porsche Boxster. She was a beauty. But when we pulled back onto the lot, we drove by the green Grand Am, and my undying love for Pontiac shouted inside me that I needed to test-drive one more car that day. The green Grand Am wasn't perfect, but she was comfortable, ran smoothly, and I know Pontiacs. There is comfort in familiarity that had me leave behind the Boxster for what anyone would say is an inferior model. But I did and had no regrets about it. I love my Pontiac.

And so, I stand in my birthday suit as Jacquelyn stands in hers, scooping cake batter into a pan. She uses her finger to scoop out a little bit of batter and feeds it to me. I eat it off her finger and smile. She deserves better. I have no chance with Faith, and Jacquelyn indeed is a Porsche Boxster if I need to make such a vulgar comparison. But Faith always shines brighter in the sun than anyone else ever will. Jacquelyn deserves to be with someone who she shines that bright for.

Hopefully, one day, she will shine that bright for me; I want her to. While the past three days seem to have dulled Faith a little, only time will tell if this shining down is temporary. It shouldn't be like this. It shouldn't be that someone needs to come along to make dull the shine of someone else. It should be that the person who comes along shines brighter. *One day at a time, Finn. One day at a time,* I tell myself, because any other way will just cling onto hope that is gone.

A quick shower and brush of my teeth later, and the cake is ready. We sit at Jacquelyn's dinner table that is straight out of the late seventies or early eighties: white laminate with gold trim, white metal legs that flare out at the bottom to make it look luxuriously laughable. But it's what she has and surprisingly beautifully contrasts the rest of the decor. Table and matching chairs aside, the cake is pretty good.

"I don't think I'll be able to see you tonight," I say, sipping some milk to wash down a bite of cake.

She smiles and swallows the last of the cake. "It's okay. Tonight is going to be a late night. I think a night away won't kill us." She winks at me, and it sends butterflies fluttering about my stomach.

"I still don't know what you do for a living," I pry. It's not that I care so much as the curiosity over not knowing has grown greater.

"I haven't told you yet." She reaches for more cake. "No questions, remember?"

"Yeah. I remember. I also thought the past three days might have earned me a little something," I say, finishing my milk. I stand up and head to the door. I have to leave and am not starting an argument over something so trivial right now.

"All in due time, Finn." She meets me at the door and wraps her arms around me. "Have fun tonight, and don't do anything I wouldn't do," she says through a little chuckle.

"After these past few days, I struggle to find what that might be." I go in for a deep kiss. Our lips connect, and tongues dance for a moment. I pull away and look into her eyes. I sense a bit of sadness inside them.

"Did I say something wrong?" I don't want to offend her. It was not my intention.

She shakes her head. "You're fine. Have fun. See you tomorrow, maybe?"

I nod as I walk out the door. As I reach the end of the walkway up to the door, I turn back. Jacquelyn watches me as I walk to my car. I smile and wave. She puts up a hand and casually shuts the door.

With the scenes from the past few nights playing out in my head, I think to myself that this night is going to be unforgettable. I need singles. Lots of them.

CHAPTER 12

Tattooed Dancer

I walk up to the place, the only place around that would let me set up what is sure to be a truly epic event, a bar in the theme-park district that holds itself to the highest standards. Tonight, we test that standard.

From the outside, the doors and the first ten feet of windows are blacked out. A way to protect their reputation, perhaps? Or to protect the eyes of innocent bystanders passing by? No matter the reason, it gives us more privacy. The bar inside is fully stocked with only top-shelf liquors, none of that Barton's or Montezuma shit. Only the best, like Cabo Wabo®, Herradura®, Casa Dragones®, Ciroc®, Belvedere®, Grey Goose®, Bombay®, Hendricks®, Havana Club®, Brugal®, and then more scotch, bourbon, and whiskey than I can even think to name. They all line the shelves for tonight's event. Opposite the wet bar is the food bar, set up with only the best Florida has to offer, which isn't a whole lot. I'm not saying there isn't good food down here. But there's no real Chicago-style dogs, Italian Beef, or deep-dish pizza. No authentic New York pizza or Cajun food.

What we do have in Florida are the best burgers in the South and possibly the country. (Some will argue that Kuma's Corner® has better burgers, but they've also been around longer.) We have Adler's Burgers at one station. From the first bite to last, these burgers put a smile on my face. The food alone creates an atmosphere of relaxation and conversation. A must-have for the night. Next to them is the Fish & Chip shop. Hands down the best in the area, and greasy food is excellent in helping break down alcohol. And of course, Tijuana Flats is set up buffet style. But what good would all that food and drink be without a dessert station? And because it's a night of lust and gluttony, we have alcohol-infused ice cream, and yes, the alcohol will add to your drunken buzz this evening. From Raspberry Limoncello to Chocolate Caramel Whiskey, Bourbon Stout Vanilla and more, there is something for everyone.

But if I am to mention all the food and drink, I can't leave out the highlight of the evening—the center stage for which all of this was set up, twenty by twenty, and stabilized with a top section to support the stripper pole. Chairs line the stage. And all of this is for us tonight. The only strange men here tonight will be us. No random creeper to make the dancer uncomfortable. Tonight, we are the random creepers. Tonight is for Gregg, to celebrate his life and his decision to tie the knot with the one girl I never thought I could respect: Jeanine.

Before any of the night's events can begin, I must do something I've been putting off. Once this night is over, even having the discussion would be counterproductive. So tonight it is. I invited Gregg out for a drink. Not here. He's not allowed to see the venue beforehand. He has no idea what is in store for him. I invite him for a pre-game drink on The Porch of Bad Decisions. I figure this is as good a place as any. Plus, we get to look out past the lake in the center of CityWalk to Toothsome® and Hard Rock® Cafe. I want to make sure that this talk I'm having, borderline too late, with him is as nonconfrontational as possible, something I am generally not one to consciously avoid. I figure though that, in this case, such precautions may be called for.

"Jeanine told me to expect this," Gregg says.

"I knew she would. She loves you. Or at least the idea of being in love," I say. So much for nonconfrontational.

"I'm gonna put a pin in that remark for a minute," he starts. "She's not Yoko. And do you know why your comparison is crap?"

I know why. But I'm gonna humor Gregg anyway. "Why?" I ask.

"'Cause by the time Yoko came along, the rest of the band was already starting to turn on itself. That piece of information is not some dark secret. Just the simple truth behind the myth that is the Yoko effect," Gregg rattles off.

"I know all that. But it's the myth that has been the root of band destructions. The band needs you, your decisions, not someone else's. Jeanine said she wouldn't interfere. I need to know that is the case and will be the case when you're on tour and she's not with you. She'll need to know you are still there for her, still with her. And I've seen it more than a few times where the female inserts herself in controlling ways as a way to delude themselves that the band member still loves her," I start.

"Jeanine's not like that," he defends.

"Maybe not now. I'll grant you that. But I need to know that a month into the tour, you won't be asking the band to change the setlist and record it as a way to show her you love her," I continue. I need him to understand and be sure.

"I wouldn't do that. Even if I did, why would it matter?" Gregg asks, starting to get defensive.

"Because it interrupts the flow. The groove that you will fall into. Change the setlist, change the groove. Friday's setlist is different from Saturday and Sunday, but they stay the same for a while. It's your first long-legged tour, and you need a groove. You need a clear mind and nothing weighing on it. No guilt from her or the band. No feelings of inadequacy because someone has injected themselves so deep in your life that you can't make your own decisions," I say, trying to wrap it up.

"Things will be fine. Once the wedding is over, all this stress will vanish, and I'll be able to concentrate on the tour," he says. "Let's pull the pin out for a moment. You said she was in love with the idea of being in love. What the fuck is that?" Anger swells in his voice.

"Let's slow down a moment. Jeanine said something about everything changing after the wedding. It came across very naïve," I explain, hoping it quells him a bit.

"So, she's a little naïve? What's the harm in that?" he asks.

Out of the mouths of babes—a thought I'm glad does not escape my lips. But I do need to respond to that question. Hypothetical, it was not.

"Look, I ran this course with Jeanine, and I'm here to make sure stuff doesn't blow up. She thinks that everything, all problems, all future problems, and any thought you might have to unzip your pants for another woman will magically get cured after the 'I do's' and refused to be told otherwise," I say as the look on his face drops. It's a look you see on someone the first time they discover something about their paramour that is less than appealing.

"I didn't realize," he says as his thoughts escape him.

"Look, I've known her since she was knee-high to a leprechaun. She's grown and matured as a human. In many ways, she's one not to reckon with." I pause for a second to make sure I said that right. I can never remember if it's "to reckon with" or "not to reckon with"; either way, I think he understands.

"But the two little words don't change anything. I'll still be on tour. She'll still be home. There will still be girls trying to cash in on some rock 'n roll fantasy," Gregg says in harsh realism.

"And I told her you're not like that. I told her you are not who I used to be." I let out a small laugh.

He looks at me with a half-smile, shaking his head. "No. Thank God I'm not. No offense, while who you were was awesome, that's just not my scene. After a show, I want to shower, maybe grab a drink at the bar with the band or crew, then crawl into bed to watch some TV."

"Have you told her these things?" I ask.

He nods his head. "I'm sure of it. I love her to death. She's my everything. I wouldn't do anything to her like that."

"Then tell her. Tell her you are the man she knows you to be and not the man she's scared you'll become." That's as honest a statement if ever there was.

"At the end of the day, Gregg, I have to look out for the band and its members. That includes you. The well-being of Spear Fist is my job," I assure.

"She's told me so many stories about you from back in the day," he starts.

"And it's stories like those that have painted all musicians to be like me. Caused her to believe that anyone in this profession must naturally act as I acted. Show her that you're not like me. Tell her what you told me and don't do what I did. You have a chance to have something great, but don't try to get there by ignoring the issues simmering below the surface." I try once again to wrap things up.

"Thank you," he says.

"Don't thank me. Just be good to the band. They're your family, at least until this tour is over. Then if you want to reevaluate your standing, you can. But the guys like you and you fit in. Don't ruin a good thing," I finish as I stand up. "You have a party to get to."

Most of the guests have arrived. The music is pumping, the alcohol is flowing, and two of the three dancers are dancing. I stand next to the bar, watching as D.B., Vincent, Neil, and Gregg are all stage-side, laughing and making it rain money down on the girls. The other attendees, friends and family of Gregg and the guys, are relatively evenly split between the stage, the food, the alcohol, and the ice cream. Hell, Ronnie's making his way through all the food as if it's about to run dry. The lights around the bar are flashing their various hues of reds, blues, yellows, and all the blended colors between.

As the song ends, one of the dancers slides off stage, picking up her bikini on her way out so the other girl can do her solo show. She heads my way as though she had been spying me while performing. I take a sip of my watered-down bourbon as she finishes dressing; a feat that done while walking must be quite tricky.

"Enjoying the night?" she says, breaking the ice.

I try to be a gentleman as I figure she is around enough sleazebags, but I do find my eyes wandering a little bit.

"It's okay," she continues. "You can look. It's why you paid us tonight."

I smile because I know that as much as men would like to think women don't notice, they do. They always do. Women don't have ESP or anything, but men harbor this illusion that women can't see their eyes wander as they look around, as if there's some law of nature that says because men can't see their own eyes, neither can anyone else. But they do; women see.

"And if you were up on stage, I'd be looking," I respond. "But you're trying to talk with me. That puts you in a different setting."

She waves her hand haphazardly through the air. "If only others were as enlightened as you."

"If only," I laugh. "So, you need a drink? Well, wait. Are you allowed to drink?"

Her eyes are still on me as she turns her body toward the bar. "I dance naked on a stage and grind on random guys' laps, and you think drinking isn't allowed? As long as I can do my job, I can have a drink." She waves down the bartender. "Vodka tonic rocks. No lime," she orders with a confidence that says this is the only thing she likes to drink. She turns back to me. "Love the tonic but never understood the old crooners and their gin. I just can't do the juniper taste."

"To each their own. If you're hungry, grab some food too," I offer up, still trying to figure out if she came here for me or for the drink.

She nods. "I will. How about a private dance? You are the one who put this all together, no?"

"Yes, I am. But I'll have to pass on the dance. Not that you aren't attractive; you are. Just that…" I start.

"You aren't sure where you and your woman stand on this sorta thing. No worries. I've seen your kind before. Your kind usually doesn't have the dough to put something this size together though," she says, sipping her drink the bartender just set down.

"If only my life were that simple."

She raises her glass. "To simple things."

I raise my glass, and we toast.

"Not to be a buzzkill but aren't there supposed to be three of you?"

She nods. "Running late. She'll be here shortly."

"She's not the only one running late," I say, feeling my phone buzz in my pocket. "Excuse me for a moment." I slide right on my phone as I make my way to the exit. "Viv! Where are you?!"

I manage to make it outside and away from the establishment to a not-much-quieter spot to try and hear her.

"I need someone to come get us! My car broke down! I can't get anyone to answer their phone!" she says in a faux panic.

"No worries. Let me tell someone who is sober enough to remember, and I'll be on my way. Do I need to call a tow truck or anything?" I say, easing her worry that she might not be able to see some strange tonight.

After finishing up the details of the where and how with Viv, I head back into the venue to find D.B. I figure letting someone know I'm leaving is better than just cutting out. D.B. is on stage, and the third stripper has arrived. The other two are dancing on the side of D.B., who is lying flat on his back. The third is squatting over his face, with her back to us, as she picks up a twenty off his nose without using her hands. I watch as she slowly lowers herself down, her wonderfully shaped derriere on display for all to enjoy. There's a familiarity to it though. A body part as ambiguous as that has a familiar look to it. I watch as she wiggles over his nose and slides on down, just enough to keep the twenty secure in her lady parts. She stands up, grabs the twenty, and turns to face my general direction.

I think of all the moments in my life that I've been shocked, awed, amazed, disappointed, dumbfounded, kerfuffled, and speechless, this one takes the cake. The face that accompanied the strangely familiar behind is one I have spent much time with as of late, and one I didn't expect to see up there—Jacquelyn—though this does explain her secretiveness about her profession. Her eyes meet mine, and in an instant, I see them go from empowered woman in control of herself and her future to ashamed girl whose father caught her doing the naughty in his home office while working out her daddy issues with some random guy.

I'm not sure what to think. There's a sense of betrayal that I feel while her eyes are locked on mine. Did she think I would belittle her for her job? Is she so used to men running away from her when she tells them she's a dancer that she felt some need to hide it? Or am I the one being naïve? Did she hide it so she could use me to get her rocks off? Please, I'm in the music industry. Hell, there's no difference between what she did to me and what I did to others. In para-phrasing the immortal Sir-Mix-A-Lot, "use and abuse me cause Finn Fairlane is not your average groupie." But still, she played me, if it was all an act like she was Little Miss-Understood. So, I gave her space and time, knowing she did her research on me and that violated the rule she set into place of no questions. She played me and played me well. Hard feelings? We shall see.

Most of the guys here are too caught up in the display of flesh that they don't notice the events transpiring around them. Most of the guys didn't notice, but Ronnie notices. I see him sipping a beer, silently watching this unfold with a sense of empathy in his eyes.

The internal thoughts that just played through my head gave Jacquelyn enough time to walk this way. Now it's time to test her mettle.

"It's hard to tell people. They all judge. You see it in their eyes," she says, standing full monty in front of me. I guess if there's ever a time for vulnerability, naked is it.

"Do you see it in mine?" I ask as bluntly as I can.

She stares at me for a moment, trying to find her answer within me. "Finn..." she starts but doesn't finish.

"You broke the rule. You knew who I was," I interject, not exactly sure where I'm going with it. "Did you think that little of me? Or was this all some game?"

I see the defensiveness overtake her. Her eyes lift up and narrow a little, like a hawk searching for prey. "A game? A game?!" she repeats a little louder. "Yes, there are those of us who think of this as one giant game and are out for themselves. Those of us who see a mark and schmooze them up to get as much money as they can without regard for what they do to get it. Is there anything I've done since we've been together that would make you think I'm after your money?!"

"I never said you were money-grubbing, and it's not my fault you've been doing this long enough that that's where your mind automatically goes. I meant our time together. Did it mean anything, or was it all just a way to pass the time between nights on stage?" I notice Ronnie inch his way toward us.

"Isn't that what you've done? For all those years, all those girls, isn't that what you've done? Isn't that what life is? Trying to find someone to help pass the time?" she retorts like some late teen trying to wax existential while sitting in a late night coffee shop. She's well into her twenties and should be smarter than this.

"There is not a woman I slept with that I wasn't in love with, even if it was just for the night. But this isn't about them. It's about you and me. Do we actually have something or not? It's a simple question," I ask as the look in her eyes calms down.

"Yes. But I didn't tell you because I didn't want to see that look in your eye that I saw." There is a steeled calm in her voice as she looks back to the stage.

"I only had that look because you never told me. I have to pick up some people. I'll be back." I find myself trying to prematurely wrap things up again this evening.

"So, I just hop back on stage and do my thing?" Jacquelyn tries to play the moment off as if nothing happened.

"Yeah. Otherwise, I'll have one disappointed bachelor on my hands. I'll see you soon." I turn to leave, and she heads back on stage.

Ronnie, who's witnessed the whole event steps over, beer still in hand. "You okay?"

I nod my head. "I think."

"Interesting girl you got there," he says, sipping his beer.

"Harsh light to see her in," I say.

"I know what you mean," he says with far more maturity and subtlety than one would expect from him. "I'll come with you. Keep you company."

"Didn't know we were good like that." I am honestly surprised at his kindness.

"We're finally even," he says, gulping down the rest of his beer. As we head out the door, he leaves his glass on a window ledge. "Let's go."

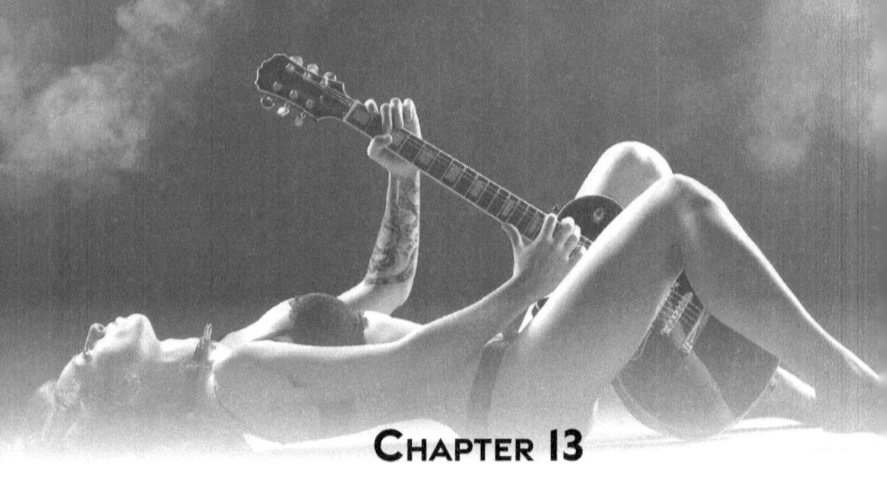

CHAPTER 13

End of Days

I feel like Orlando is listening to me, empathizing with me at this moment. The confusion, pain, and frustration the city and I feel are manifested in the chaotic rainfall and gusting winds that sweeping across I-4. The city is telling me it understands. It knows what I feel, and it feels the same. While rain is not an unheard-of occurrence in Florida, these rains are harsh for this time of year. Not a true tropical storm, nor a hurricane, at least not that anyone has told me about. This storm brewed quickly. The skies showed no warnings while I talked with Gregg earlier, but now it rages on. Even on high, my windshield wipers can't keep up. At least the traffic isn't at a standstill. The sounds of Okilly Dokilly playing from my phone connected through the auxiliary jack keeps us company in the storm.

"Not a good feeling, huh?" Ronnie says. I will give him this; he might not be an intellectual on many levels, but he gets straight to the point.

"It's … not pleasant," I respond. The last thing I want to do is piss off a monster who has finally called a truce. "I perhaps let my past take control of my better senses. It wasn't the proper thing to do."

"That's over, bro. You have new problems." He again shoots the bullseye.

"Yeah. I do." I try to smile. The thought of Jacquelyn hiding this from me is really what strikes a nerve. God knows I've done enough in my life not to judge her for her career path, but hiding it, even after she broke the agreement and researched me, that's what irks me.

There's a small part of me that says, "So what? She's a stripper. Get over it." I want to get over it and be fine. But if she knew who I was and am and still decided to hide it from me, then there must have been a reason. First thought would be shame, but I didn't see any in her eyes. I didn't hear any in her voice. So, I have to figure out what I am missing. I have to find the disconnect in my mind that makes everything all right.

"So?" Ronnie asks as the rain continues its relentless assault.

"So what?" I say back.

"So, what ya gonna do about it?" He lays it out.

I have nothing to tell him. I don't think my mind has gotten past the initial shock and anger of finding out in such a manner. I'm a grown adult and hold no illusions about the fairer sex. I know she's had sex and other sex-type relations with people before I came along. Hell, who hasn't by her age? I don't judge her by her past or present as she doesn't judge me for mine. But despite all that, the sight of her sitting on D.B.'s face is burned fresh into my mind. It's not an image that holds any amusement or humor for me. At least not right now.

If I force myself to stop and reason for a second, I don't care that she's a stripper. I don't even care she hadn't told me yet. I care that circumstances were as such that I found out what she did for a living by seeing her wrap her crotch around my friend's nose to pick up a ten spot or whatever it was. Then again, if I was a Dancing Bear and she found out while some lady was swallowing my sword to the hilt, I'm sure she'd be upset too. So, I guess, in the end, it is kinda funny. At least it was D.B. and not some creepy stranger. Of course, now I'm imagining her surrounded by a bunch of wrinkly, old men, all half-chubbed and dry-humping themselves while tossing five spots her way. But I push these images out of my mind and turn my attention back to the road and conversation.

What am I going to do about it? Hell, I don't know, but I do know that while this might seem like some big, defining moment in our, or any, relationship, it doesn't need to be. This isn't going to ruin a good thing, not something like this. It'll take something much more significant to destroy it for us.

"I'm going to be okay and move forward with us," I say most politically. "You can't expect people to change once you already accept them for who they are."

"Not to play the devil's advocate but you didn't know that about her to have chosen to accept it before you guys … whatever…" Ronnie lets his thought trail off, as if that many words strung together at one time, and using the phrase "devil's advocate," overheated his brain.

The music playing through my phone is interrupted. I look down at the caller ID and, for the first time since the night we met, wished she hadn't called. The rain has kicked up a few notches, rendering the high-speed wipers useless. I don't have time to reach down to my phone and reject the call before Ronnie swipes answer, putting it on speaker.

"Hey, Faith. What's goin' on?" I say, trying to keep it casual.

"Oh, hi," she says, sounding startled that I answered my own phone. "I was expecting voicemail. Aren't you at Gregg's bachelor party?"

"I'm picking up Viv and Logan. Viv's car broke down," I reply.

"Well, I guess in person is better than voicemail anyway," she starts.

"Okay but..." I try to tell her Ronnie is with me.

Faith interrupts, "No. I gotta say this."

Ronnie and I exchange glances. I raise my palms in defense for a quick second, then return them to the steering wheel as the car starts to pull right. He raises an eyebrow.

Faith continues with her thoughts. "I tried telling you the other night, but Ronnie interrupted."

Again, Ronnie looks my direction. This time, the raised eyebrow is replaced by gritted teeth, a look I've seen before and don't want to feel the end of, especially while driving.

"But Faith," I try again to interrupt.

"No, Finn. I'm not going to be brushed off or interrupted. I have something to say, and I'm going to say it."

I pick up my phone to take it off speaker, but before I can, she speaks.

"I'm pregnant." She finishes her thought.

I drop my phone onto the floor. The auxiliary cord tugs a bit as my foot kicks the phone farther out of reach. As I reach down to grab it, I swerve into the left lane. I grab the phone and return to my lane. A smooth recovery for such roads.

Ronnie throws his hands to the air. "You're what?!"

A startled Faith can be heard stammering on the other end of the phone. "R-R-Ronnie?!"

The traffic ahead all slam on their brakes. A jagoff in the right lane thinks this is the opportune time to cut in front of me so he can be ten feet farther in the dead-stopped traffic. The wind and rainy conditions exaggerate my swerve to avoid the collision with said-jagoff, and I find myself starting to hydroplane into the left lane. I steer into the skid but pull halfway into the lane next to me. I unwillingly force the car next to me onto the shoulder, but the conditions are too much for the sudden merge. His car hits the median and bounces back. As I regain control of my vehicle, the bounce off the median causes the other car to collide with my driver's side front tire.

"Faith!" I call out as my car spins, smashing the passenger side and Ronnie into the jag that cut me off. I hear a smash of glass as Ronnie's head shatters the passenger window. My car continues spinning another half circle. Ronnie slumps forward.

I try to catch my breath through the pain of the crash. The dead-stopped traffic in front of us is unscathed by my hydroplaning spinout. But the car that got run off the road isn't as lucky. I see out my windshield as the car gets hit, causing the start of a small pileup. A large passenger truck jerks his wheel to avoid the pile-up but is headed dead for me. The only thing standing between the inevitable impact of the truck and myself is Ronnie.

I look to Ronnie. He is still leaned forward, unconscious. A stream of blood flows down from the right side of his head and down his chest. The passenger door window is shattered.

My eyes are fixed on the truck barreling toward me. My ears take in the sounds of the rain and blaring horns. Somewhere, buried with the sounds of the chaos, I hear Faith crying out my name. "Finn! Finn! What's going on?!"

But I can't call out to her. I hear her call my name over and over. All I can do is watch as the truck helplessly slams into the passenger side of my car. In a split moment, I see the metal crumble, and the force of impact pushes Ronnie almost on top of me. His head falls toward me. My car shifts a few feet. I can feel it slide on the wet pavement. I only stop sliding because the car on the other side of mine is pressing its bumper into my back.

I know I can still feel my legs. I know because I can feel Ronnie's blood run down them as it streams out of his head. My chest hurts. Each breath is a struggle for air.

"Faith!" I whimper out. My voice gets drowned out by the sounds of the highway and rainstorm.

"Finn! I can't hear you! What's going on?! Where's Ronnie?" Her frantic yells fill the air.

I look down and see the phone. As I reach down for it, a stabbing pain grips my ribs. I cry out in pain. I can't reach it. I must have broken a couple of ribs. My back hurts. I can still feel all my limbs, which I assume is a good thing.

Ronnie is slumped toward me, blood still trickling out of his head. The crimson puddle below him and sprayed all around tells me he's lost a lot of blood. I look to what remains of the passenger side door. The metal and fiberglass are crushed. His seatbelt suspends him in position. He needs help, if it will still do any good. I need to get help.

I force myself to unlatch my seatbelt and reach for the phone. As I do, I hear a loud cracking sound and feel a ripping sensation from my rib cage. My scream echoes through the phone to Faith.

"I've called 911, Finn! Stay with me!"

I look down to my ribs and see a bone jutting through the skin. Blood starts to trickle out of the wound. It doesn't appear serious, at least not compared to Ronnie.

Each word I say is a struggle. A fight for the air to speak. "Faith. It hurts. So bad. Ronnie's. Not moving. Bleeding. Everywhere."

"Help is on its way. Finn, I love you! Stay with me."

The pain is too much. The world around me starts to fade. I try to concentrate on the sights and sounds, but all my mind can do is think that Faith said she loved me. That has to be something. That has to be enough. I think about Ronnie, the guy next to me. The guy who is actually with Faith. Why isn't he moving? What happened in the initial impact that's causing so much blood? I guess, in the end, it doesn't even matter. His bleeding has slowed down. I no longer feel the blood running down my leg. I don't see it dripping off his head.

She said she loved me. I heard her say it. She loves me. It shouldn't take harsh realities like this to bolster the courage to say such vulnerable words. Three little words. She has told it to me before, and every time there were always excuses that followed. Reasons that even though she said she loved me, we couldn't be together. Anything to run and hide from the way she felt, from the fear that gripped her of the possibilities of what is and what could be. She always ran. Here, now, she has given me a reason to hold on. A reason to "not go gently into the night," as Dylan Thomas said but to stay here. Hang on to everything I have as long as I can. I know help is on the way. She told me it was. She wouldn't lie to me.

I concentrate as the world continues to fade. The noises that surround me start to grow distant, like a fading carnival as you drive away. The rain seems to beat down softer than before. The searing pain from the snapped rib has dulled down. I hear sirens in the distance. Maybe all will be okay.

The story continues with
The Fragile Finn Fairlane

Books in The Fairlane Series:
The Fairlane Incidents
The Fortunate Finn Fairlane
The Fragile Finn Fairlane

Other Books by Nick Savage:
Us of Legendary Gods
So We Stay Hidden
The West Haven Undead

Coming Soon:
World Whore, D

ABOUT THE AUTHOR

Nick Savage lives in the greater Orlando, Florida area with his wife and two cats. Besides writing, he enjoys making music and art and playing video games.

4HorsemenPublications.com